The initial stabbing jolt of fear lasted a half beat before she relaxed and smiled. Obviously this was a dream—because no man had a face like that.

It was a master class in perfection, Miranda decided as she studied the shade and shadow of the dark fallen angel before her. Sharp angles and strong curves made this a face that went beyond mere symmetrical prettiness.

She stared, feeling an almost physical tug as she looked into velvety dark heavy-lidded eyes fringed by long, spiky lashes.

It was some moments later when, with a small sigh, she let her gaze stray to the fantasy mouth, its sculpted lips somehow managing to be stern and overtly sensual at the same time. The small crescent-shaped scar a few centimeters from the right corner of that extraordinary mouth was startlingly white against the uniform toasty gold of his skin, somehow emphasizing how perfect everything else was.

"Good morning."

Her eyelashes fluttered against her sleep-flushed cheek. Like the face, the voice belonged in a dream. Deep and throaty, it even had the tantalizing hint of an accent. The man with broad, taut, heavily muscled shoulders, a dark shadow on his square jaw, was the sort of man many women's dreams were made of...though he seemed awfully real for a dream...and wasn't she awake?

Though lacking much authentic Welsh blood, **KIM LAWRENCE** comes from English/Irish stock. She was born and brought up in North Wales. She returned there when she married, and her sons were both born on Anglesey, an island off the coast. Though not isolated, Anglesey is a little off the beaten track, but lively Dublin, which Kim loves, is only a short ferry ride away.

Today they live on the farm her husband was brought up on. Welsh is the first language of many people in this area and Kim's husband and sons are all bilingual—she is having a lot of fun, not to mention a few headaches, trying to learn the language!

With small children, the unsocial hours of nursing didn't look attractive, so encouraged by a husband who thinks she can do anything she sets her mind to, Kim tried her hand at writing. Always a keen Harlequin reader, it seemed natural for her to write a romance novel—now she can't imagine doing anything else.

She is an avid gardener and cook and enjoys running—often on the beach, as living on an island the sea is never very far away. She is usually accompanied by her Jack Russell, Sprout—don't ask, it's a long story!

Other titles by Kim Lawrence available in ebook:

Harlequin Presents® Extra

181—IN A STORM OF SCANDAL
157—A SPANISH AWAKENING

Harlequin Presents

3027—THE PRICE OF SCANDAL
2984—BEAUTY AND THE GREEK

GIANNI'S PRIDE

KIM LAWRENCE

~ Protecting His Legacy ~

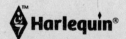
™ Harlequin®

TORONTO NEW YORK LONDON
AMSTERDAM PARIS SYDNEY HAMBURG
STOCKHOLM ATHENS TOKYO MILAN MADRID
PRAGUE WARSAW BUDAPEST AUCKLAND

Recycling programs
for this product may
not exist in your area.

ISBN-13: 978-0-373-88245-8

GIANNI'S PRIDE

First North American publication 2012

Copyright © 2012 by Kim Lawrence

www.Harlequin.com

Printed in U.S.A.

GIANNI'S PRIDE

CHAPTER ONE

IT WAS eleven, a good two hours later than he had anticipated arriving, when Gianni eventually pulled up in the beat-up borrowed four-wheel drive. All things considered, he had decided with regret that the low-slung, sleek, powerful sports model that he enjoyed driving was not really a man-plus-child sort of vehicle—not only did young children not travel light, they were poor respecters of cream leather upholstery—and the rather more upmarket version he used to ferry his son around town was in for a service.

Besides, this was meant to be a low-profile trip; he was dropping off the radar for—if Sam was true to her word—a few days. It could not have come at a worse time from a business and personal perspective.

It was considered something of an honour to be asked to give the keynote lecture at the prestigious international literary festival—the previous year the honour had gone to an ex head of state. After pulling out at the last minute as a mere head of a publishing house, no matter how globally success-ful a brand it had become, Gianni doubted this ac-colade would be coming his way any time again soon! He had hopes that the lovely young model he had had to cancel on would be more forgiving but if not...there were other models.

He glanced into the back seat. His son had been asleep five whole minutes—five minutes of blissful silence apart from the worrying knocking noise in the ancient engine. No crying, no howl-ing, no pathetic whimpers and, most importantly, no throwing up! A self-derisive half-smile twisted the sculpted contours of his hard mouth as Gianni reflected on the distinctly patronising note in his response when Clare, Liam's nanny, had expressed doubts about undertaking the journey without her.

'It's late, he's tired—he'll probably sleep most of the way. While I accept you're indispensable, Clare, I think I can muddle through. Enjoy your holiday.'

Humouring her, he had accepted the proffered travel bands and even half listened to her lengthy explanation of how they should be applied to the pressure points on Liam's wrists to lessen nausea, and then he'd tuned out a great deal of the rest of the advice she gave while privately thinking, *How hard can it be to strap a sleeping four-year-old child into the back seat of a car and drive a hundred miles?*

He shook his dark head. He was just glad now he hadn't expressed these views out loud or he would be feeling more of a fool than he already did. He also wished he had not left those travel bands on the table in the hall or given in to Liam's requests for a burger and fries at the first rest stop. It had been all downhill from there.

Gianni winced now to recall his flippant parting shot.

'Yes, Gianni, definitely a piece of cake,' he muttered under his breath as he unclipped the harness of his son's booster seat, trying hard not to inhale—the wet wipes supplied by a sympathetic woman in the last motorway services had not removed *all* the smell. Gianni scooped the sleeping child into his arms and nudged the car door closed with his knee, wincing as it banged loud in the still night.

'Don't worry, kiddo, it's bedtime,' he murmured as the whiffy bundle in his arms gave a cranky protest.

The picture-postcard thatched-roofed house, a white blur against the copse of trees behind, was in darkness. Presumably Lucy, who habitually rose at some unearthly hour to feed the variety of livestock and strays she had accumulated during the past two years, was already in bed. Seeing no point in waking her, and anyway in no mood to hear her inevitable amused critique of his parenting skills—his aunt never had a problem when it came to calling a spade a spade—he made as little noise as possible as he walked across the gravel. Then, balancing Liam on one arm, he reached for the key Lucy kept on the ledge above the door.

The moonlight appeared from behind a cloud as the red-painted door swung inwards, the silvery light illuminating the hallway enough to enable Gianni to make his way upstairs without switching on the lights. After depositing Liam on the bed in the small single room in the eaves of the house, he headed back to the car to grab the bag of essentials that Clare had packed for her charge, before hurrying back.

Liam had not moved an inch. Holding his breath and crossing everything crossable, he gingerly peeled off his son's soiled clothes. To his relief the boy remained flat out, his breathing soft and even as Gianni replaced them with a pair of fresh pyjamas—a bath would have to wait for the morning. Smoothing the strands of dark hair back from a hot, sticky brow—the poor kid was utterly exhausted—a frazzled Gianni paused, the hard lines of his handsome face softening as he stared down at the cherubic sleeping features of his son, feeling the familiar rush of pride and fierce parental protectiveness.

That he had had any part in producing something so damned perfect still filled him with a sense of astonishment and awe. It might not have been planned, but fatherhood was the best thing he had ever done and from the moment of his birth his son had become the centre of his universe.

Carefully folding down the heavy top cover—it was a warm night—he opened the leaded window a crack, pulled the curtains and cast a last glance at the sleeping child, stifling a yawn as he finally headed for the adjoining room and his own bed. Halfway there he paused. If Lucy woke before him an explanation for the unknown vehicle parked in her yard might be a good idea. Lucy, who had once been the most trusting person on the planet, had reason to be suspicious of strangers. A note, he decided, should do the trick.

The dogs asleep in the kitchen rose to greet him half-heartedly as he went in, rubbing against his legs as he propped a suitable missive up against the cereal box on the big kitchen table. Neat freak Lucy, it seemed, had relaxed a little if the general clutter on the normally pristine work surfaces was any indication. He patted the dogs and made his way back to bed, checking on the sleeping child on his way there.

Ten seconds after Gianni's head hit the feather pillow he was asleep. It was the sunlight shining through the window that awoke him.

Where am I?

The feeling of disorientation lasted only a moment; it was then followed by another—not so momentary.

This was a first.

He was thirty-two and though there had been some moments in his life he would prefer to forget, none up to this point had involved waking up with a total stranger in his bed.

And she was a stranger because that hair would not be easily forgotten, he decided, momentarily distracted by the remarkable shade of the thick mesh of curls, Titian interwoven with copper threads, spread out on the pillow beside him.

Raising himself on one elbow, he studied the slender back of the sleeping woman, who lay with one arm curled under her head, the other draped over the patchwork quilt. His glance travelled from the unvarnished neat nails up the curve of her arm. She had a redhead's skin, pale and milky, lightly dusted with freckles along the curve of her shoulder and the nape of her neck where there had been sun exposure.

As far as he could tell she was naked. If anyone had walked in now they would assume… Was that what this was about—some sort of elaborate scam…?

The cynical furrow between his dark brows

smoothed as he rejected the half-formed theory. *Getting paranoid, Gianni*, he told himself.

His eyes narrowed in effort as he kick-started his brain into sluggish life. *Think, Gianni...focus... first, ditch conspiracy.* This couldn't be a set-up— nobody knew where he was. This he had made damned sure of. Gianni had tracked down enough people who had wanted to disappear to know that a secret stopped being a secret the moment you shared it.

That left...?

That left a big fat zero. Who was the naked woman with the silky-looking skin? His dark gaze caressed the smooth curve of her shoulder. *Really silky...focus, Gianni!* More important than identity was why was she here and in his bed?

Except it wasn't *his* bed, was it? And it wasn't his house.

His deep-set almond-shaped eyes framed by long thick black lashes widened as an explanation occurred to him. Was it possible the girl had been in the bed when he had climbed in too tired to register the warm body lying beside him?

Not only possible, you idiot—probable!

Presumably waking and finding a stranger in her bed would not be a good way for her to meet Lucy's house guest. Gianni felt a stab of irritation. Obviously he was glad that Lucy had decided to take his advice and stop being a total recluse—he just wished that she hadn't got sociable just yet.

He reached carefully for the quilt, curling his long brown fingers around the edge as he kept a cautious eye on the sleeping woman. Removing himself from the bed before she woke up was definitely desirable. His narrowed gaze left her briefly to make an impatient sweep of the room. Where had he left his clothes last night…?

Caught half naked in a woman's bed. Gianni could see the tabloid headlines now and none of them said innocent mistake!

He spotted his clothes, but too late—at the same moment the sleeping figure yawned and stretched luxuriously, the sinuous catlike movement sending the sheet slithering lower to reveal the dip of her slender waist and feminine flare of her hips below.

Gianni winced, then, about to slide out from under the quilt, paused, fatally distracted as his eyes were drawn against his better judgement to the smooth, slender, womanly curves, lingering on the suggestion of a dimple above the swell of taut, peachy buttocks. Then the moment was gone—she murmured something and began to roll over, tugging the quilt up to her chin and snuggling down.

Gianni inhaled and prepared himself for the worst. Always, in his opinion, a good idea—a man could always be pleasantly surprised.

Let's just hope she has a sense of humour!

In the event she didn't scream. After blinking like a sleepy kitten, she smiled in warm, sleepy invitation—or maybe she was just short-sighted. Either way, lust bypassed the logic channels in his brain and Gianni caught his breath and lost his sense of urgency.

She was beautiful.

As usual Miranda woke sixty seconds before the alarm was set to go off. This morning it had been set to go off early. Her house-sitting duties involved more than the feeding of the family pets she had imagined and, having a strongly developed work ethic, she was determined to fulfil every task that her new employer had outlined so meticulously in one of her lists—there were a lot of lists.

The menagerie all had names that were not quite sorted in Miranda's head yet: the ancient horse, the Shetland pony and the donkey, even the ducks and hens. Her employer had jotted down the list in her own neat hand. She had jotted a lot down, including a cleaning schedule that to Miranda, who didn't mind a bit of clutter, seemed a little excessive, but she was being paid, and paid quite well, for having what her dad had called a holiday. That was before she had admitted that actually she wasn't going back at the start of the new term; she had handed in her notice. Her *paid holiday* had then become a demeaning job for someone with her skills and qualifications.

Miranda sighed and wriggled a little deeper into the soft mattress, refusing to replay the argument in her head. She was escaping, not running away. The distinction was important and her actions long overdue... *Think positive.*

Although she hadn't welcomed it at the time... Oh, all right, she had pretty much felt as though the sky had fallen in on her head and she still couldn't bring herself to say it was a good thing, but if it hadn't been for her sister Tam sweeping the man Miranda had wanted to grow old with off his feet things could have gone on as they were indefinitely, with her cutting a pathetic figure hoping that one day Oliver would notice she was something other than a dependable teacher of domestic science.

No, not dependable, exceptional, Miranda silently corrected in line with her new philosophy of 'if you've got it, flaunt it'. If she'd flaunted her not at all bad figure in the sort of designer clothes that Tam wore it was possible that Oliver would have noticed more than her raspberry muffins.

Heartbreak aside, Miranda realised she actually felt good. She normally had a problem sleeping in a strange bed but last night she had gone out like a light and, apart from some strangely realistic dreams that were already slipping away, she had slept through the night. Perhaps it was a good omen.

Eyes still closed, she rolled over towards the window set in the uneven wall where the age-blackened exposed oak beams stood out dark against the bright blue paint. There were a lot of bright colours in the cottage. It had been a combination of the view across the rolling countryside from the window and those beams that had made Miranda select this room when Lucy Fitzgerald had said she could choose any one she liked—that and the enormous, hedonistically soft bed with the carved wooden headboard.

'Lush,' she murmured sleepily under her breath as she snuggled into the layers of feather mattress. Her right hand brushed the headboard, her left touched warmth and hardness… Still half asleep, she slowly turned her head.

The initial stabbing jolt of fear lasted a half beat before she relaxed and smiled. Obviously this was a dream because no man had a face like that.

It was a masterclass in perfection, Miranda decided as she studied the shade and shadow of dark fallen-angel features, fascinated by the sharp angles and strong curves that made this a face that went beyond mere symmetrical prettiness. This face represented a perfect combination of planes and hollows, the masterful nose aquiline, the razor-sharp cheekbones high and slanting, the forehead broad and intelligent. Miranda stared, feeling an almost physical tug as she looked into velvety dark heavy-lidded eyes fringed by long spiky lashes and set beneath strongly delineated ebony brows.

It was some moments later when with a small sigh she let her gaze stray to the fantasy mouth, the sculpted lips somehow managing to be stern and overtly sensual at the same time. The small crescent-shaped scar a few centimetres from the right corner of that extraordinary mouth, startlingly white against the uniform toasty gold of his skin, somehow emphasised how perfect everything else was.

'Good morning.'

Her eyelashes fluttered against her sleep-flushed cheek. Like the face, the voice belonged in a dream. Deep, throaty—it even had the tantalising hint of an accent. The man with broad, taut, heavily muscled shoulders, the dark shadow on his square jaw, was the sort of man many women's dreams were made of… Though he seemed awfully real for a dream and wasn't she awake…?

Miranda blew away a curl that was tickling her nose, smelling the musky, spicy scent of warm male and a hint of some sort of male fragrance…. Expensive, she decided. He was an expensive dream man. Her eyes brushed the stubble on his square jaw, following the curve of his sensual mouth. He was also raw and raunchy. Personally she was more into subtle and sensitive when it came to dream men.

Or one dream man. A smiling image of Oliver drifted through her head, a billion miles from raw or raunchy. Her lips parted to release a wistful sigh. Miranda had met her dream man, worked with him on a daily basis and accepted that he just didn't think of her that way... Then oddly it turned out he did see her sister—identical twin sister, how was that for irony?—that way.

Miranda prided herself on the fact that she had been grown-up about the situation, concealing her pain so well that Tam had remained oblivious to her heartbreak, and avoiding the dreaded knowing looks and sympathy. Even when, on the day before the wedding, her sister had confided that she was pregnant Miranda had somehow said the right thing, though she still had no idea what. She had actually begun to wonder if she had not gone into the wrong profession—she should have been an actor, not a teacher. But there were limits and Miranda knew she'd had to make a break—working in a school where Oliver, now her sister's husband, was the headmaster was a non-starter.

While she and Tam had never shared the sort of empathic link that Miranda had read some identical twins enjoyed, there was no way even her twin, who was never that interested in things that did not directly involve her, would not catch on soon.

She directed her masochistically inclined thoughts from the imagined idyll Tam was enjoying on a Greek island with her bridegroom and concentrated on the man lying beside her. Now he was *definitely* raw—actually raw hardly covered the smouldering, in-your-face sexuality he exuded from every pore... *The man she was looking at?*

There's a man in my bed!

Her horrified gasp was drowned out by the alarm clock that began to shrill. It stopped when she lobbed it at the strange man's head and in a seamless motion, her sleepy contentment a dim memory, produced a stumbling exit from the bed modestly wrapped, in the best tradition of old movies, in most of the bedding.

Eyes like saucers, clutching the quilt to her heaving bosom, she stared at the man lying there, trying not to think about the draught that was cooling her exposed bottom. The adrenalin in her veins was telling her to run, but to get to the door she had to get past the bed. Thoughts racing, hyperventilating dramatically, she glanced longingly towards the open door that connected with the next room, but her feet remained nailed to the spot as she was submerged by a massive wave of visceral, paralysing fear.

Attack, they always said, was the best form of

defence… Act like a victim, she had read somewhere, and you became a victim.

'Don't move an inch!' *Or what, Miranda?* Her
chin lifted, the defiance in her attitude an attempt
to mask her fear as she played for time, waiting for
her legs to move. 'Or y-you'll r-regret it!'

He had to have heard the quiver of fear in her
voice…but on the plus side he hadn't made any
attempt to move. If he had… Miranda's glance
slid down the long, lean length of the stranger.
Even in his present recumbent position his physical superiority was pretty apparent. His lean body
was heavily muscled, not an ounce of spare flesh
masking the power and vitality of a man at the
peak of physical fitness.

He looked like the sort of fitness fanatic who
could run marathons back to back without breaking sweat. He could swat her like a fly if he wanted
to… Swatting was actually the least of her worries at that moment… Refusing to speculate on
his intentions, she tried to breathe past the frantic
pounding of her heart as, not taking her eyes off
him, she surreptitiously reached out behind her for
her phone. She could remember leaving it on the
bureau the night before… Hadn't she?

CHAPTER TWO

ONE hand pressed to his eye where the alarm clock she had lobbed as she exited the bed—not before he had got a glimpse of a lovely pert little bottom—had landed a glancing blow, Gianni looked at her through his uncovered eye and held up his free hand in a gesture of surrender. It did not take a genius to figure out what she was thinking.

'Relax. This is a simple misunderstanding…a mistake…' he soothed, making eye contact and experiencing a flicker of shock as he registered the quite extraordinary colour of her wide long-lashed eyes.

Extraordinary enough to make him briefly lose focus—an event in itself for the ultra-controlled Gianni—the deep, dark green made him think of cool, quiet forests, and the tiny flecks of amber recalled dappled sunlight shining through the foliage as she stared at him as though he were a coiled snake about to strike.

'You mistakenly climbed in through the window

and mistakenly took off your clothes and mistakenly got into my bed… That's a lot of mistakes.' Mine might be not keeping my big mouth shut, she thought as, picking up some of the slack of the quilt that trailed on the floor, she threw it awkwardly over her shoulder. Her rear now concealed by a heavy fold of fabric, she continued to feel exposed, just not to the elements.

Was the husky little rasp in her voice normal or a product of fear? Either way the tactile quality was extremely attractive, so much so that Gianni found himself curiously impatient to hear her speak again even if it was to hurl some more abuse.

'When you put it like that it does sound bad,' he admitted. 'But I really am totally harmless.'

Do not hyperventilate, Miranda!

Struggling to maintain her hard-fought-for air of bravado, she sketched a tight little smile and thought, *Sure you are…* Anything *less* harmless than the man sprawled there like some sort of macho centerfold—after registering he was wearing nothing but an insubstantial pair of boxers she had kept her gaze above the waist—would have been hard to imagine.

He oozed sinister sexuality and was probably insane to boot! A predatory man had climbed into her bed… She shuddered—had he touched her…?

Her stomach responded violently to the lurid

images forming in her head. 'God, I think I'm going to be sick!' she groaned suddenly as she dropped her chin to her chest, the blood draining abruptly from her face.

Her voice made even this prosaic statement sound seductive! 'I'm getting that a lot.'

The dull metronome *thud thud* of her blood as it pounded against the delicate membrane of her inner ear drowned out his dry words.

What had Lucy said before she left…? *I hope you won't be bored. I'm afraid nothing interesting ever happens here.* What would her employer call this—a slow Friday morning?

'This is all an innocent mistake.'

She inhaled a deep sustaining breath and lifted her head, fixing the intruder with a look of loathing. 'Do you say that to all the women you try to molest?' Amazingly her voice was steady, if on the shrill side.

Miranda's fingertips brushed the phone before she heard it fall onto the polished boards—damn! Her teeth clenched, she fought down the panic she felt closing like a fist around her windpipe. *I will not be some crime statistic. I'll survive.* 'I'm going to leave now.' *Once I regain control of my limbs.*

'I'm not stopping you.' People feared his tongue, words written and spoken were his thing, and Gianni had rarely encountered a situation where he did not have the perfect response, but then up until now he'd never been viewed as a potential rapist. He found himself falling back on repetition.

He watched her eyes flicker around the room like a trapped animal seeking an escape route. 'I've told you, this is simply a misunderstanding— a mistake.'

'Yes, your mistake.' How come her voice was working and her legs were not? The other way around would have been much more convenient. 'You disgusting sleaze!' *How come I am saying the sort of things almost guaranteed not to placate a dangerous lunatic?* 'I know self-defence.'

He could see her shaking from here, her eyes didn't leave his as she watched him, but she had guts, this redhead. Terrified, she still came out fighting. Gianni felt a stab of admiration as he pulled himself into a sitting position.

The action caused the petrified redhead to take a hasty step backwards.

Gianni, who did not like scaring women, produced a smile and struggled to channel harmless and innocuous—not so easy when you were a powerfully built six feet four and practically naked—as he studied the woman hiding behind the quilt she had dragged off the bed, along with half the blanket and sheets that now lay crumpled at her feet, and tried to figure out the best way to defuse the situation.

She was petite and slim and probably younger

than Lucy. Though it wasn't always easy to tell, she had the sort of face that looked perennially young—good bones, he decided, studying her delicate heart-shaped face dominated by a pair of enormous green eyes set above a neat little tip-tilted nose. Noticing that she had a kissable mouth that would be soft and lush when it wasn't curled into a scared snarl was not going to defuse anything, but it was impossible not to. It was the sort of thing any man could not fail to notice.

'There's absolutely no need to freak out this way.'

He actually had the cheek to sound vaguely impatient. Her trill of laughter emerged husky from her bone-dry throat. If ever a situation called for major freaking, this was it!

'I'm not freaking.' She had gone beyond freaking!

'This isn't what it looks like.'

'So what the hell is it?' she snarled, looking so spooked that he was afraid she'd do something crazy like jump through that open window if he made a move to leave. Then, accident or not, her beautiful broken neck would be his fault.

'Look, there's a bathroom next door with a really sturdy lock on it. Why don't you go in there, lock the door and we'll sort this out?'

Not the sort of suggestion you might expect a potential rapist to make... Miranda did not lower her guard, but her anxiety levels dropped from red to amber. 'How do you know that the bathroom has a lock?'

Thoughts continued to chase one another in frantic ever-decreasing circles around her head. Was this all part of some sinister plan? Was he playing with her...? Had he cased the joint while she slept? And what about the dogs? Lucy had said they barked at strangers.

'Did you hurt the dogs? Because if you have... they're rescue animals and...'

'I know, they've had a bad time.' Aunt Lucy had typically taken on the most tortured, hopeless canine souls she could find. 'The dogs are fine,' he soothed, thinking, *For animals that their owner refuses to discipline.* 'Just yell Lucy, she'll vouch for me.' He raised his own voice and bellowed. 'Luce!'

Taken by surprise, Miranda blinked. 'You know Lucy?' That had to be good, didn't it?

Gianni tilted his head in confirmation and raised his voice in another bass bellow. 'Lucy!' Before adding in a conversational tone, 'I really had no idea she had a visitor.' His dark brows twitched into a sable line of irritation—where was Lucy? If his yell hadn't roused her it had to have woken Liam. 'Luce!'

'She isn't here.' She stopped, trying to conceal a stab of dismay as she thought, *Way to go, Mirrie!*

If he didn't already know you were alone, he does now. And he might indeed know Lucy, but he was still pretty much an unknown quantity and one not to be trusted.

His dark brows twitched into a straight line above his hawkish nose. 'She's away?' He released a hissing sound of annoyance through his clenched teeth and thought, *Just my luck. When was the last time Lucy left this place?*

'But she'll be back any minute.'

The tremor in her voice brought his scrutiny to her face. His dark eyes held understanding as he lifted his broad shoulders in a shrug.

The action made her unwillingly aware of the movement of muscles under the satiny surface of his dark skin. He had the sort of body that would have an artist reaching for a pencil. He had the sort of body that she could imagine incited a less artistic and much more hands-on response!

'Look, I'm sorry I scared you… It came as quite a shock to me too to find I was sharing.'

'I'm not scared,' she lied. Unable to stop her eyes straying to the fuzz of dark hair sprinkled across his magnificent pectoral muscles, she swallowed. The man might look as if he were posing for some cheesy calendar, but he exuded an earthy, raw quality that was not cheesy so much as downright disturbing. 'How did you get in?'

'I let myself in with the key. Lucy keeps one

above the door on a ledge… Yes, I know, crazy when she's gone to all the trouble of installing a state-of-the-art security system, but she works on the theory that nobody would ever look in such an obvious place, and in answer to your previous question I know about the bathroom lock… I know where the key is kept because I've been here before…'

'*Before?* Are you her boyfriend?'

The suggestion drew an unexpected laugh, deep, throaty and attractive. 'I'm family.'

This time it was Miranda who almost laughed. She might just have swallowed boyfriend, though that would beg the question of why he'd climbed into this bed and not the one in the roomy, pretty master bedroom at the front of the house.

Actually it was not hard to see this man, with his Mediterranean colouring and bold eyes, and Lucy Fitzgerald together as a couple, she mused as she studied his rather too perfect profile… Individually either would stop conversations when they walked into a room. Together they would definitely cause an earth tremor…but family? No way, she decided. Lucy, with her cut-glass accent, was fair-skinned with incredible blue eyes and masses of ash-blonde hair that looked natural. This man, with his bold black eyes, ebony hair and bronzed body, was dark and not just in colouring. There was something elemental and primitive about him…volatile…dangerous.

'Family?'

He tilted his dark head in acknowledgement. 'I arrived late and I didn't want to disturb anyone so… I use this room when I stop over, even though I've had the odd concussion when I've forgotten to duck.'

He looked sincere, the story sounded genuine, but then she had continued to believe in Santa Claus right up to the moment her more sophisticated twin had disillusioned her a good two years after her contemporaries. Repressing her natural instincts towards annoying gullibility, she struggled to retain a protective level of scepticism. 'If you say so…'

'You're a tough audience, you know that, don't you? Did you see the photos downstairs?'

Miranda, who had registered the large collection of framed photos on the dresser in the dining room, maintained an uncommunicative silence, but began to consider the possibility he might actually be telling the truth about the relationship.

'You noticed them?'

She tipped her head in wary acknowledgement. 'So what are you—her brother?'

He took her sarcasm at face value. 'No, her nephew.'

'*Nephew?*' She gave a derisive hoot. 'You've obviously never even met Lucy.'

'You base that on what?'

'Well, let me see, for one she's younger than you, and English and you…I don't know what you are! But I think you heard she was away, thought you'd see if there was anything worth taking, saw me asleep and—'

'Could not resist the temptation…?'

Miranda felt the colour scoring her cheeks deepen.

'While I don't like to boast, it has been known for a woman to voluntarily share my bed,' he admitted mildly. 'As for my relationship with Lucy, she is my aunt, and, like her, I'm half Irish. My other half is Italian, hers is English. Lucy is two years younger than me and she is my aunt. Grandad Fitzgerald had three wives and ten children. My father was his oldest and Lucy, who came thirty years later, his youngest.

'Look at the photos,' he suggested. 'You'll see me in at least two of them…not flattering likenesses but…' Holding her eyes the way he would a spooked horse, he put his feet on the floor and added in a soft voice, 'If I was going to lie I'd come up with a much more convincing story, *cara*.'

Miranda maintained her defensive pose. He looked no less dangerous but on the other hand he had a point: his story was just lame enough to be true...

Gianni produced a smile that Miranda struggled not to respond to.

'Sling me that shirt and pants, would you? They're on the chair.' Actually they were on the floor. He ran a hand down his hair-roughened chest before letting it rest on his ridged and muscled belly. 'I'm feeling slightly self-conscious here.'

Now that was a lie!

Miranda, whose eyes had followed the movement of his hand from his broad chest to his washboard-flat stomach, lifted her gaze abruptly. Anyone more relaxed about being scantily clad in front of a stranger would be hard to imagine. She, on the other hand, was painfully conscious of her state of undress and even more painfully conscious of his!

Not *totally* convinced by his story, but no longer feeling he represented a physical threat to her, she kicked the shirt his way, waving her foot in agitation as it caught on her bare toe. Danger gone, her embarrassment was kicking in big time.

Gianni bent forward and picked it up, flashed what Miranda recognised as a grin of practised charm her way and shrugged it on. 'I'm Gianni Fitzgerald, by the way.'

Miranda ignored both the unspoken invitation

to introduce herself and the hand he extended her way. She had less success ignoring the ripple of muscle beneath his satiny skin that accompanied his every action.

After a pause Gianni shrugged. 'So where is Lucy, and when is she actually due back?' He arched a sardonic brow. 'Or is that classified?'

'She's in Spain.' Miranda aimed her response to a point over his shoulder. At least he was putting on some clothes, which was a good thing. The bad thing was that standing there with her modesty covered by the bedding left her feeling no less vulnerable than before.

Standing on one leg, a very long, muscular and hair-roughened leg—not that she was looking—somehow he made the action as he thrust the other into the leg of the crumpled jeans she had kicked across look effortlessly elegant. Prone to clumsiness, she had always envied coordinated people.

'Why has she gone to Spain?'

If her employer had wanted to tell this Gianni, presumably she'd have told him. Respecting Lucy Fitzgerald's right to her privacy, Miranda said vaguely, 'She might be back in a month.' Actually it was vague—the arrangement had been left pretty open-ended, with Miranda assuring the other woman that she could stay as long as she was needed.

Gianni dragged a frustrated hand through his

hair and slid his second leg into the jeans, tugging them up over his narrow hips, zipping the fly, but leaving the leather belt threaded through the loops hanging loose.

His bronzed chest lifted as he sucked in a deep breath and released it slowly. Lucy being absent was not a possibility he had taken into account. He'd been relying on lying low here to give Sam the breathing space she had begged. 'We have a problem.'

'We?' Miranda shook her head at the inclusion; she had enough problems of her own without being included in those of a total stranger.

CHAPTER THREE

'DADDY, I want a drink…'

Daddy…? Miranda's head turned in the direction of the crabby childish voice.

Her jaw fell and her astonished eyes grew as wide as saucers as she registered the small figure standing in the doorway. He looked to be around three or four, was wearing a pair of pyjamas emblazoned with a cartoon character and clutching a stuffed toy that might once have been a rabbit in his hand.

Her accusing glance switched back to the man who called himself Gianni Fitzgerald. 'He's yours?'

Gianni nodded.

Miranda's attention switched back to the child, who stood there rubbing his eyes with a clenched fist. His lower lip stood out as he walked across to his father and repeated his demand.

'I want a drink—'

'Please,' his father inserted automatically.

Dear God, how heavily had she slept? How many other people were asleep in the house?

'You're not Aunty Lucy!' The child directed an accusing look Miranda's way from eyes that were, she saw immediately, the same unusual piercing blue as Lucy Fitzgerald's, his hair was as dark as his father's, the rosy-cheeked, sun-kissed face feature for feature a childish version of the older man's.

It looked as if Gianni Fitzgerald really was who he said he was and also some things he hadn't said he was! Things like married and a father.

Admittedly these were not necessarily the first things that someone said when they woke up and found themselves in bed with a stranger. Nevertheless, on behalf of women who might be interested, and she was guessing there might be more than two or three, a man who was spoken for in her opinion should wear a wedding ring.

Her glance flickered towards his long, brown tapering fingers. He had the hands of a musician or an artist; they were ringless.

Despite the fact that she knew she could now relax—this really had been what he claimed, a mistake, and even if it hadn't been, a man intent on violent crime did not in general bring his child along—Miranda found herself clutching the blanket tighter. She no longer thought she needed to protect her virtue from a dangerous lunatic, but she might still die, only now from sheer embarrassment!

'No, I'm not, I'm Miranda…Mirrie.' She forced a smile for the child. 'And you're…?'

'Careful there, champ,' Gianni said, reaching out a hand to steady his son as he climbed up onto the bed. 'This is Liam. Miranda…?' Dark head tilted a little to one side, he studied her as though deciding if the name fitted; after a moment he nodded approval, so presumably it did.

Miranda turned her head away, aware that his scrutiny had brought a bloom of awareness to her cheeks. She had never encountered a man who had the trick of making the most innocent gesture…intimate.

'Hello, Liam.' Her smile faded and her green eyes acquired an unfriendly frost as they moved towards his father. 'You didn't tell me you weren't alone.'

Gianni's ebony brows arched sardonically. 'Is that your version of, "I'm sorry, Gianni, I can see now that you were telling the truth— it was a genuine mistake"?'

'Me apologise to you!' The words were startled from Miranda.

'Well, you did assume some very unpleasant things and I have provided you with a dinner-party story that will just give and give.'

She tried not to smile at his martyred expression. The only thing that made his arrogance tolerable—almost—was the fact he appeared to have a disarming sense of humour.

'I think,' she replied with dignity, 'that I had some justification…like waking up and finding you in my bed…?' As for sharing this incident for the amusement of her friends, Miranda could not at that moment conceive of circumstances when she'd feel like sharing this story.

'I was mildly surprised myself, but I gave you the benefit of the doubt. Innocent until proved guilty is my motto.'

'Well, don't worry, you're quite safe from me,' she told him with a sniff before adding crossly, 'Didn't it occur to you to explain who you were right off and mention that you had your son with you?'

'I didn't get much opportunity.'

'I'm very, very thirsty,' the child, who was trying to run up and down the bed, complained. 'And I want to go home. I want Clare—she always leaves me a glass of water by my bed in case I get thirsty in the night.'

Who was this Clare? Miranda wondered. And where was the child's mother?

'Clare isn't here.' Not the best decision he'd ever made, but then hindsight was a marvellous thing. 'It's just you and me.' *Piece of cake,*

Gianni—those words were really coming back to haunt him.

'She's here.'

The child waved a hand towards her, and Miranda took an involuntary step forward in alarm.

'He's going to fall,' she warned, holding her breath as she watched the dark-haired boy sway precariously as he ran up and down the bed, coming close to the edge. His father did nothing. 'Shouldn't you…?' She lifted her eyes to Gianni's face and as she encountered a distinctly hostile expression her voice faded.

Gianni's square jaw had tightened several notches in response to an attitude that he had plenty of experience of, an attitude that never failed to get under his skin. He was in a position to know that being female did not necessarily make a person a childcare expert and having a Y chromosome did not make him utterly clueless.

'He's not going to fall.' Gianni's confident pronouncement coincided with his son landing on his bottom on the polished boards.

With a cry Miranda moved in to help but the boy's father, who had responded with much quicker instincts and a lot more agility, had dropped to a crouch beside the boy, hiding him from her view.

He might be pretty clueless about long journeys with a child prone to car sickness, Gianni reflected, but at least he did know enough to keep anxiety out of his voice as he asked lightly, 'Are you all right—hurt anywhere?'

Liam was inclined to laugh off bumps and bruises unless he picked up on an adult's anxiety—then things could tip over into hysteria.

There were tears in the limpid blue gaze that lifted to his father. Gianni smiled reassuringly and ran his hands lightly down his son's body to check for any obvious injuries.

The boy blinked several times and bit his wobbling lip before he shook his head and said, 'I'm fine… Fitzgeralds are tough.'

Gianni patted his son's shoulder and gave a thumbs-up sign as he rose to his feet. 'Good man.'

Miranda, who had watched the revealing interchange with a disapproving frown, was forced to swallow to clear the emotional lump in her throat when the boy returned the thumbs-up gesture and beamed with pride as he struggled valiantly to his feet.

This was a very appealing kid who obviously wanted to please his father, who was clearly a paid-up member of the macho 'boys don't cry' school of thought.

She just hoped for this child's sake that his mother provided a softening influence. *If ever I have a son,* she thought fiercely, *I'll teach him that a boy is allowed to have feelings. He's allowed to cry.*

'You haven't said I told you so yet.' Gianni turned his head and arched a sardonic brow. Caught unawares, Miranda found herself pinned by a heavy-lidded cynical stare.

'I haven't said big boys don't cry either,' she fired back, unable to totally shake the illogical feeling that those mocking eyes could see right into her head.

One corner of his mouth lifted in a mocking smile. 'Are you suggesting I'm not in touch with my feminine side, Miranda?'

Miranda was startled to hear him use her name with such familiarity. The way he said it made it sound...*different*? 'N-no...' On another occasion the suggestion might have made her laugh—feminine? The man who oozed more testosterone than a rugby team!

'I'm half Italian, half Irish—neither are known for their inhibitions when it comes to expressing emotions.'

Miranda looked at the sensual curve of his mouth and thought, *I can believe it.*

'Frequently loudly,' he admitted with a flash of white teeth.

Miranda turned her head quickly to break the hold of his mesmeric gleaming stare and, ignoring her violently quivering stomach muscles, directed her attention to the little boy. 'Are you sure he's all right?'

It was the child under discussion who responded to the question. 'No, I'm not all right. The car made me sick…a lot,' the little boy announced with a hint of pride. He gave her a look resembling a mistreated puppy—it would have melted stone—and said pathetically, 'The car smells. Daddy was mad.'

'Was he? I'm sure that helped a lot.' The smiling comment passed over the child's head but hit its target.

Reconciled to being considered the monster in this scene, Gianni shrugged and thought, *Why fight it?* 'A man and his car—you know how it is.'

Miranda gave a scornful snort, edged a little towards the window and glanced down seeing, not the shiny boy's toy his comment had brought to mind, but a disreputable-looking four wheel drive parked down below.

You could tell a lot about a man by the car he drove, as her mother had always told her daughters—her theory was not in Miranda's experience foolproof, but sometimes dead on. Oliver drove a solid estate, which suited him; safe, steady and dependable.

'Gracious!' she exclaimed. 'I'm not surprised he was sick in that thing! What possessed you to transport a child who suffers from travel sickness in something that's one step up from a horse and cart?'

'You know what they say, Miranda—beggars can't be choosers,' he drawled with a languid shrug. 'And I'm obviously not the expert on all things relating to childcare that you are.' Jaw clenched, he arched a sarcastic brow. 'How many children do you have?'

'That's not Daddy's car. Daddy has a big, big car!' the child boasted as he made a thrumming sound in his throat and began to charge around the room in imitation of a car, proving if nothing else that he hadn't been injured by the fall.

Miranda's softly rounded jaw tightened with annoyance. 'I don't have children and I never claimed to be an expert.'

'Just a woman.'

'What have you got against women?'

His sensually sculpted upper lip curled into an exaggerated leer. 'I have never been accused of not liking women.'

I just bet they like you right back, she thought, dragging her gaze from his mouth, aware as she did so of the heavy ache low in her abdomen. This man really was sinfully attractive. She felt a spasm of sympathy for Liam's mother, then as her eyes were drawn back to his mouth that vanished as it occurred to her the woman didn't need sympathy—she had that mouth.

Rather shocked by her thought, she blinked, then lowered her gaze, balling her fists on the quilt as she resisted the sudden impulse to touch her own lips.

'I'm sure that makes your wife deliriously happy.'

'I'm not married.'

'Oh, I thought…' Her eyes moved in an unscheduled sweep from him to the playing child and back again. Not married did not mean they were not a couple.

He answered the question she was clearly gagging to ask. 'No, we are not together.'

'Oh!' What was she meant to say to that? After an awkward pause she produced a lame. 'I…sorry.'

His expression froze. 'Do not be. Liam does not suffer in any way because his parents are not a couple.' By the time he was old enough to think about it, few of Liam's friends would be the products of a conventional family unit.

But how many would have a mother who had declared herself unwilling and unable to adjust her lifestyle to accommodate the needs of a child?

As always Gianni pushed away the thought. It was a question for the future and he would deal with it at the appropriate time.

The same way he'd dealt with Sam's initial bombshell when she'd told him she was pregnant; the same way he had dealt with her sympathetic but amused response when he had asked when she was going to give up front-line journalism—the days of speaking calmly to a camera while bullets whizzed by her were clearly to his mind over.

His only experience of mothers was his own and she had put her family first, and while he had never expected the mother of his children to turn into some sort of fifties stay-at-home housewife—he had no problem with her having a career, just not one that involved being held hostage by rebel bandits—it had not crossed his mind that she would not be the main carer.

Just as it had not crossed his mind that he would not be married to the mother of his child.

Startled that her reply had elicited such a defensive aggressive reaction, Miranda thought, *Wow, did I hit a nerve or what?*

'Liam is—' Gianni stopped, the groove between his brows deepening as he realised that, for someone who was not in the habit of discussing his personal life with strangers or defending his actions to anyone, he was doing a pretty good impression of someone who needed approval.

Lowering his dark lashes in a lush veil over his eyes, he ran a hand over his jaw where a dark shadow of the stubble that gave him a vaguely piratical air was visible. 'I don't enjoy arguing before I shave or have my first coffee, especially with naked women.'

The sly addition caused Miranda's hand to fly to her mouth. Bad idea because the quilt slipped on one side, almost causing a dramatic wardrobe malfunction—or as dramatic as a B cup could be.

One corner of his mouth tugged upwards as Gianni watched her struggle. 'It gives them an unfair advantage.'

Unfair! For a moment she was rendered totally speechless—the nerve of the man! Miranda, who had never felt at more of a disadvantage in her life, scowled before arranging her features into an expression of mock consternation.

'Well, I'm all for a level playing field, and I wouldn't want to be accused of taking advantage, so in the interests of fair play we can continue this conversation when I've got some clothes on.'

His laugh was warm, deep, throaty and totally unexpected. Miranda, aware of a faint responsive quiver low in her stomach, fought the urge to smile back. She knew he was a man who spent his life smiling and having people—women—smile back.

Miranda could think of few things worse than being with a man every woman lusted after, unless of course it was having the man you loved fall for your twin sister!

'That seems fair,' he conceded. 'Come on, champ, I think a bit of soap and water might be appropriate.' He scooped up his son, his nostrils quivering at the stale acrid smell. 'I left the bags in the kitchen. How's about we take the bathroom downstairs and you take the one up here—the one with the big lock.'

At the mocking addition she lifted her chin, pushing away the mental photofit image in her head of a beautiful long-legged blonde hanging on his arm and keeping out a constant eye for the opposition. 'And don't think I won't use it, Mr Fitzgerald.'

He laughed again, but this time just with his eyes. God, but the man had bad boy written all over him—she had never been attracted to bad boys, though that seemed to put her in the minority.

'My mother warned me about women with smart mouths.' But they had no discussion on mouths that were made for sin, he thought, his darkening glance lingering a moment too long on the lush curve before he turned and walked towards the door, grinning but not turning back when she yelled after him.

'And my mother told me that men who are afraid of smart women generally have self-esteem issues.' The effect that brief heavy-lidded stare had on Miranda's nervous system had been nothing short of electric. Breathing hard and trying not to hear the rich throaty sound of his amused laughter, she struggled to shake off the weird lingering feeling of anticipation and excitement heavy in the pit of her stomach as she lifted her makeshift robe and walked towards the bathroom.

CHAPTER FOUR

MIRANDA used the lock with an air of defiance, not caring—actually hoping he would hear it slide home. He might be innocent of knowing she was in the bed when he got in—that much she accepted—but she imagined it was one of the few things that Gianni Fitzgerald was innocent of!

Father to a cute child or not, he had the air of a man who had no problem crossing lines. Parenthood did not make him harmless—not that she expected for one second that he'd test the lock. Gianni Fitzgerald was not a man who needed to batter down doors if he wanted female attention; all he had to do was smile…or laugh… The echo of that warm sound sent a little shiver down her spine.

She dropped the quilt on the marble floor, warm with the under-floor heating that was a feature of the entire cottage, and turned on the shower. Instead of stepping into the vast double cubicle— Lucy Fitzgerald had spared no cash when it came to the luxurious renovations on this farm cottage—she leaned back against the door, closed her eyes and waited for her heartbeat to return to something approaching normal.

It continued to bang against her ribcage, the echo loud in her ears for a long time. The encounter had left her on a high. She knew it was the effect of adrenalin, but as she struggled to tamp down the weird combination of exhilaration and antagonism circulating through her veins the scene played on a loop in her head.

Finally with a sigh she levered herself upright and walked into the shower, gasping a little as the cool needles of water hit her warm body. Face raised to the jets of water, she reached for her shower gel and began to lather her skin, rubbing until her body tingled, but Gianni Fitzgerald's voice lingered, along with his slow, sardonic smile, the mixture of insolence and amusement in his attitude and the sensuality that came off him in sonic waves.

When she emerged a few minutes later she felt satisfied she had washed Gianni Fitzgerald out of her hair figuratively speaking, now she had to do it in the practical sense and reclaim the cottage.

After towel-drying her hair she pulled on the clothes she had grabbed from the top of her case. She was short of a bra, but that wasn't a major problem. She was not exactly over-endowed in that area and the fabric of the denim-coloured cotton shirt she fought her way into was not exactly clingy. Her still-damp skin felt oddly sensitive as she hurriedly buttoned it up.

She was dragging a comb through her thick, damp curls when from below she heard a bang and clatter. The kitchen, to her way of thinking the most impressive room in the cottage, was located directly underneath this room.

Her brows twitched into a frown as she glanced into the mirror, connected with her overbright eyes and looked away again quickly.

What was he doing now? she asked herself when there was another loud bang. Mingled with the dismay she experienced at the thought of any breakages was a stab of real concern. Kitchens could be dangerous places for little boys.

The kitchen in the cottage was at the back of the house. It opened out on to the courtyard of stone outbuildings. She had spent a happy hour exploring the large room the night before, discovering that the free-standing rustic-looking units hid some very unrustic state-of-the-art shiny appliances that had not come cheap. Clearly money was not an issue for Lucy Fitzgerald; though there was no clue in the place as to how she made her living, the woman herself had offered no information and Miranda had not liked to ask.

'I don't cook,' the beautiful blonde had admitted when Miranda had expressed her admiration for the room.

Miranda, secretly scandalised by the indifference—it seemed a criminal waste of a kitchen she would have lived in, given the chance—admitted she enjoyed cooking.

'Well, the freezer's full of ready meals, but if you want to cook anything from scratch go for it,' her employer had offered, pulling open the door of a well-stocked store cupboard that made Miranda's eyes widen and saying vaguely, 'There's stuff here. A friend brought in some things—I was going to teach myself the basics.' She gave an attractive self-deprecating grimace and admitted, 'But I never actually…well, anyway, feel free. There's a local farm shop and a terrific fruit and veg man who calls… Quite cute actually, if you're not spoken for…?'

Miranda admitted she was not but did not go into detail and the other woman, respecting her privacy, had not pushed it.

Pushing away the memory of the conversation with a lot more success than she had had with the surreal events of this morning, Miranda squared her shoulders and reached for the door handle.

She walked in at the moment Gianni Fitzgerald tipped a dustpan full of broken crockery into one of the neatly labelled recycling boxes set beside the open stable door. Liam was sitting on a kitchen chair swinging his legs and patting the head of one of the dogs, a shaggy lurcher.

The child's dark hair was damp, his cherubic face shiny and clean. He looked wholesome and delicious. His father, who also had damp hair, did not look wholesome, but he did look delicious.

Rampantly delicious, she decided, taking the opportunity while unobserved to work out what it was beside his startling male beauty that made her skin prickle when she looked at him—and she didn't even like all that macho stuff! Miranda told herself that it was simple scientific curiosity that made her want to study him, though it was hard to call the hollow achy feeling in the pit of her stomach scientific.

She swallowed to ease the tightness in her dry throat. She couldn't think she was the only female whose brain shut down in his vicinity—presumably Gianni Fitzgerald produced a similar visceral response in any female with a pulse. Was it the Latin thing…? Half Italian, he'd said, but she could see precious little of the Celtic heritage he had claimed in his dark toned features. His dark hair slicked back from his broad brow was still wet. The sleek style emphasised the beautiful severity of his lean, hard-boned, classically proportioned face.

Dressed casually in a loose-fitting black tee shirt—the loose cut did nothing to disguise the lean, muscular torso she knew it covered—and faded jeans that clung to his long, muscular thighs, he oozed a raw sexuality that had nothing to do with what he was wearing and everything to do with the man himself.

As if feeling her gaze, Gianni turned his head. Caught staring at his bottom, Miranda lifted her chin to an angle of mute defiance and adopted a 'so hang me' expression that made his mouth quirk slightly at the corners as he tipped his head in silent acknowledgement of the gesture and allowed his dark, long-lashed eyes to travel in a slow, comprehensive sweep up from her toes until he reached her face.

At this point their glances connected and Miranda, who had been enduring the scrutiny, glimpsed something that moved like silvered fire deep in his midnight-dark eyes.

She could not define what she had seen, it had only been there for a fraction of a second, but her body wasn't dealing in names. It reacted indiscriminately, sending a wave of scorching heat through her body.

Whatever this man had, clothes were no protection, she mused as she tugged fretfully at the neck of her shirt, unwittingly loosing the top two mother-of-pearl buttons.

Gianni's eyes went to the deep vee of milk-pale smooth skin revealed, hardly what could be termed provocative, but his body responded with a disproportionate pulse of hunger that slammed through his body before concentrating in a hard ache of frustrated desire in his groin.

He swallowed hard, annoyed by his lack of self-control, and tipped his head in exaggerated approval, resorting to strained banter in an effort to disguise his reaction while recognising an equally strong need to rationalise it.

'I hardly recognised you with your clothes on, *cara*,' he drawled, and watched the angry colour fly to her smooth cheeks.

A man woke up next to a beautiful woman and the inevitable happened. It was no mystery, nothing more complicated than physical hunger, nothing a cold shower...another cold shower would not cure.

Before Miranda could respond with a suitable degree of scorn to this worn-out cliché—it was always harder to deliver scorn when your face was the colour of a post box; this man was dangerous—Gianni's attentions switched abruptly to his son.

'No, stay where you are, Liam, until I check out the floor...' The rest of the sentence was delivered in Italian and Miranda was fascinated to hear the child clearly as bilingual as his father, reply in the same tongue.

Unexpected emotion tightened in Miranda's

throat as she watched them, the sternness leaving Gianni's face as he bent down to the chair, spanned the child's waist with his big hands and lifted him down, pushing him in the direction of the open door.

'I'm hungry!'

Gianni, whose routine meant he was out of the house before his son took breakfast—he rarely had time for anything himself other than a double espresso and a bagel—paused before reaching for the tin that he recalled sweet-toothed Lucy kept filled with biscuits. It was empty.

'*Dio.*' His long fingers beat out an impatient tattoo on the granite work surface as he experienced an unaccustomed stab of indecision and doubt. For a man who stayed cool while those around him went into meltdown it was an uncomfortable experience.

Small wonder, he reflected grimly, Clare had looked aghast when he'd told her he planned to spend some time alone with Liam. The nanny had probably wondered if she'd get the child back in one piece. It might have been better for everyone concerned if she'd come right out and said he didn't have a clue.

He sighed through his nose and squared his shoulders. His time might be better spent proving her wrong rather than feeling sorry for himself. For once he had the quality time with his son that always seemed in short supply.

'Where are the biscuits…bread…?'

Miranda watched as he looked around the room with the air of a man who expected someone to materialise and produce what he required out of thin air.

Seeing this self-assured man look at a loss actually made her feel a little less antagonistic towards him. Perhaps in his world that was what happened, Miranda speculated. He certainly had the arrogance of someone who was accustomed to giving orders and expecting people to jump.

Miranda didn't jump, but she did walk across to the well-stocked fridge and pull out a carton of milk from the shelf. Not because she felt the need to rush to his rescue, but she could hardly let the little boy go hungry just because his father was a bossy, ungrateful control freak with, admittedly, a very nice bottom and a way of looking at her that made her feel jittery and defensive.

She found the plastic tumbler she was looking for in the second cupboard she tried and, filling it, handed it without a word to Gianni.

'Perhaps that will keep him going until breakfast?'

Gianni waited for the lecture on child nutrition. In his experience it was a rare woman who could resist the opportunity to display her superior knowledge, and when it didn't come he tipped his head in silent acknowledgement.

He stood guard until Liam had finished the glass of milk before wiping the milky moustache from his upper lip and nodding his permission for him to go outside into the yard.

Positioning himself by the door so that he could keep one eye on his son, he folded his arms across his chest and watched while Lucy's house sitter began to prepare breakfast.

'Can I do anything to help?'

Miranda adjusted the flame on the grill and, still holding her hair from her face with her forearm, lifted her head. 'No.' Then, conscious of the occasions she had been accused, with some justification, of being a bit of a prima donna in the kitchen, she softened the refusal by glancing his way and adding, 'Thank you, I'm fine. I like to cook.' The least she could do was feed them; she had no idea how far they had to go.

Gianni pressed his back against the exposed stone wall, crossed one foot over the other and watched her.

'You look like you know what you're doing.' It was a strange kitchen but her body language was relaxed and she was actually humming softly under her breath.

The women he knew did not cook; hell, they did not generally eat, though they liked to sit and push food around a plate in fashionable restaurants! He was, Gianni realised, attracted to this redhead more than he had been attracted to a woman in a long time. *Recognise it and move on because it's not happening,* he told himself, unless his instincts about her were totally wide of the mark…? He studied her soft profile, hoping to pick up on something that would suggest he was wrong about her, that she was actually a woman who wanted just sex from a man and not a piece of him.

He didn't. Desirable or not, Lucy's house sitter was the sort of female he actively avoided. He was a single parent, he worked long hours in a demanding job—he thought he juggled the twin roles pretty well, but romance and all that went with it were not on his agenda.

'Yes, I do,' she admitted, not feeling the need to display any false modesty on this subject. 'But I'm making scrambled eggs,' she pointed out, trying not to be pleased by his comment. 'It's not exactly rocket science or, for that matter, Michelin-star stuff.'

'That kind of depends on your perspective. The last woman who cooked for me put a takeaway in her microwave still in the foil tray—set the microwave on fire.'

She laughed, her eyes flying wide. 'Seriously?'
He nodded.
Fighting the urge to respond to the charm in his

smile, she lowered her gaze and muttered, 'I'm making breakfast, you're here—I'm not cooking *for* you.'

And who was she cooking for? Miranda wondered. She knew his name, she knew he was related to her employer, but what was Gianni Fitzgerald other than a man prone to dizzying mood swings and owner of more charm than was good for him? He was a man with so many contradictions that it was hard to put him in a neatly labelled box—a man who drove a vehicle that looked one wheel bolt from the grave while his clothes might be casual but the labels said expensive. Not that he couldn't have made cheap look good, she acknowledged, wondering a little at her curiosity as her eyes swept upwards from his boot-shod feet, pausing when she reached the metal-banded watch that gleamed against the golden skin of his hair-roughened wrist.

'Yes, it's the right time.'

'What? Oh!' Her eyes flew to his face. 'I was just checking out...'

Amusement sparkled in his dark eyes. 'I noticed.'

'Not you! That is the time,' she gritted, feeling the flush working its way up her neck. She bit her lip, silently cursing the fair redhead's skin that came with the double curse of freckles and blushing. The blush deepened when he glanced from his wrist to the clock that had to be three feet in diameter positioned on the wall directly above her head.

'It's a nice watch…'

And if it was genuine, and he didn't act like a man who was interested in fakes, it was also worth as much as she earned in a month, maybe more.

He gave a non-committal grunt. 'Is this what you do for a living?'

She shook her head and thought, *Is this what you call changing the subject?* 'What?'

'The cooking-is-the-way-to-a-man's-heart thing.' His gesture took in the utensils neatly arranged on the butcher's block, but in his head he was seeing her pale back, the skin smooth and flawless. It would not, he conceded, matter if she burnt water. This innately sexual little redhead would never have any problem accessing if not men's hearts, certainly their libido.

She lifted her chin and tossed a smile up at him. 'Relax, I am not interested in your heart, Mr Fitzgerald,' she retorted.

'It's not my heart you have an effect on, *cara*.'

Miranda compressed her lips, not caring to be the butt of his warped humour. The annoyance in her eyes was dramatically extinguished as she encountered the smouldering heat in his ebony stare.

Not a joke!

She snatched a startled breath and felt her stomach flip before going into free fall.

'I'm flattered.'

Heart thudding, she brought her lashes down in a protective sweep. No man had ever looked at her with such unvarnished lust before.

'I studied domestic science at college.'

Miranda and her sister had been going together, though Tam's chosen subject had been fashion design, then two weeks before the start of term a chance meeting had dramatically changed the course of Tam's life.

Miranda's thoughts drifted back to the day they had been standing with their mother on the platform waiting for their train home after a shopping trip.

They had laughed all the way back on the train about the man who had given Tam and their mother his card. He had barely glanced at Miranda, clearly not seeing any potential star quality, and explained he was a casting agent for a production company.

Back home Tam had retrieved the card from the rubbish where their mother had thrown it and, unbeknown to her parents, called the number. It had turned out to be genuine and three weeks later she had successfully auditioned for a part in an American soap. The show had never crossed the channel so her sister, although an instantly recognisable face in the United States even two years after the show was cancelled, could shop at the local supermarket at home without being asked for her autograph.

'So you work in catering?'

She shook her head. 'No, I teach…taught in the local comprehensive I went to as a kid.' *Too much detail if you want the man to stay awake, Miranda.*

He wants you.

She closed her eyes for the duration of the primitive thrill that she felt all the way from her scalp to her toes.

'Not very interesting, I know.' She hated the vaguely apologetic note and could only hope he hadn't picked up on it.

He had.

'Isn't it?'

Thrown again, this time not by his blunt declaration of lust but by the direct question, Miranda blinked, then dropped her gaze from his obsidian stare feeling totally flustered.

'Not interesting compared to what?'

She was alarmed by the perceptive reasoning revealed behind his deceptively simple question and her head came up with a startled jerk. She said the first thing that came into her head, which, luckily, was not on this occasion, *Your mouth is beautiful.*

'Does Liam like scrambled eggs?'

Gianni watched as she began to whip a bowl of eggs with a hand whisk. He had clearly touched a sensitive nerve. None of his business, he told himself.

'Does he?'

Gianni looked at her blankly.

'Like eggs?'

Gianni glanced down at his son, who had wandered back into the kitchen, and replied without thinking. 'I don't know.'

She didn't say a word; she didn't have to—the look she gave him made it perfectly clear what she thought of fathers who weren't au fait with their sons' dietary preferences before she dropped down to the boy's level and put the same question to him.

Gianni's son, after a brief questioning glance towards him, gave an identical reply in a loud childish treble.

'How about if you try some and I'll give you some bacon too?' she said, cutting up a couple of crispy slices from the pan on the Aga. 'How about some tomatoes…?' The tomatoes in the greenhouse she had watered the night before had been groaning with fruit. She had picked some with the intention of making some chutney.

'Aren't you going to cut it up for him?'

Gianni, who had been about to do exactly that before his son managed to get the other half of his food on his clothes, found himself shaking his head. 'He can manage.'

She glanced towards the little boy, who was

better at handling a knife and fork than his terminally stubborn father was at taking anything resembling advice. 'I hope you brought another change of clothes.'

Her amused smile made him want to... Actually even without the smile he had found himself wanting to kiss those luscious lips. He stabbed a piece of bacon with his fork and scowled. It was not the first time he had found himself attracted to an unsuitable woman. Unsuitable in his situation constituted any woman likely to want more than he was willing or able to give, but rarely, if ever, had his body responded with such immediate urgency to a woman the way it did to this redhead.

Of course he'd like to see her naked again but it wasn't going to happen.

Dio, he saw little enough of his son as it was, and the pressure of his workload... He shook his dark head slightly as he banished the dangerous thoughts in his head—he was stretched thin enough without consciously adding emotional complications.

And she was.

You didn't have to be a psychic to see this redhead would be the high-maintenance sort of woman.

'What?' Miranda asked, waving a fork in the direction of the man who was watching her when his scrutiny became impossible to ignore. 'Has nobody ever told you that it's rude to stare?' She compressed her soft lips into a thin line, annoyed as much by the fact he got under her skin so easily as his astounding rudeness.

He rested his elbows on the table. 'I've never seen anyone your size put away that much food,' he admitted, watching her fork up another mound of golden, fluffy eggs.

'I have a fast metabolism,' she retorted, feeling like some sort of freak show. It was actually a relief when Liam knocked over his glass of juice and those dark disturbing eyes finally left her face.

When Liam had finished eating Gianni shooed him back out into the yard and helped himself to another coffee from the pot.

Miranda collected the plates and put them in the dishwasher. Aware of Gianni Fitzgerald's silent presence, she opened the fridge and put the jug of milk back inside. The day was already warm and, if the weather forecast on the radio was to be believed, set to get a lot warmer.

She struggled to keep the eagerness from creeping into her voice as she directed her casual query to the man standing at the open stable door.

'Would you like me to make you some sandwiches for the journey?'

'Journey?' he echoed, still watching Liam, who was chasing hens around the cobbled yard.

'Well, I assume you'll want to be going back

to…' Her slender shoulders lifted as she thought, *Wherever you come from.*

'You assume wrong,' he drawled, turning his head now to pin her with a look that once more struck her as cold and calculating. Under the smouldering surface and charismatic charm this man was, she recognised, cold—cold at the core. The only time that coldness was entirely absent was when he looked at his son, she realised.

A little shiver traced a path down her spine as the dark stare continued to pin her. It took a conscious effort to break the contact.

'Call me Gianni—the women who have shared my bed generally do.'

Miranda shifted uncomfortably as the colour flew to her cheeks. 'They invited you…' She lifted her brows. 'I'm assuming they invited you?'

'You seem interested in my sex life.'

Her eyes narrowed in dislike as she encountered the speculative and not very kind gleam in his eyes. 'I'm just thinking what a great role model you are for your son.'

In the blink of an eye the mocking lazy humour in his eyes morphed into narrow-eyed hostility. This man with his mercurial mood swings could, she realised with a little shiver, be ruthless.

Not the sort of person you wanted to antagonise. Knowing this, she still couldn't stop herself adding, 'It's probably just as well you're just a week-end father.'

His angular jaw tightened another notch. 'I am not a weekend father.' Just one who didn't know if his son liked eggs. 'I am a full-time parent.'

'But what about his mother?' She stopped and thought, Oh, God, have I just been as insensitive as hell? 'Liam has a mother? I mean, she is… alive…?'

'Sam is very much alive, she is just not— She has some contact with Liam but I have full custody.'

Some contact?

The clinical statement made Miranda shudder. 'How terrible for her!' It was inhuman, in her opinion, to take a child from his mother. The thought of being forced to give up your child—surely no woman would do so voluntarily—sent a fresh judder of pained horror through Miranda. 'And poor Liam…'

His dark eyes flashed fire and the muscles around his mouth quivered in reaction to the accusing condemnation in the big eyes fixed on his face.

'Liam does not need your pity,' he snarled. 'And neither does Sam. There was no coercion involved. I did not obtain custody under duress. Liam's mother did not want us—' He closed his mouth over further revelations. *Better late than never, Gianni.*

Dio, what was he doing? She was not the first person to make this assumption, but this was the first time he had felt the need to justify himself and play the sympathy card.

The simmering silence stretched until it was broken by her gruff, 'I'm sorry.'

'What the hell for?' he ground out. 'Being nosy?'

Hearing that 'us' again in her head and knowing instinctively that this man was never going to totally forgive her for seeing beyond the macho façade he presented to the world, she shook her head, wishing she hadn't. He was the last person she had imagined she could feel empathy for, but she was. It had been more comfortable to view him as a smouldering, sexy but ultimately two-dimensional figure; when he was gone her equally two-dimensional lust would be gone too.

No worries—soon he would be and she could get back to feeding the goat and, what? Feeling sorry for herself? Wasn't that what she had intended to do? Instead…the guilt switch in her head clicked and her lashes moved downwards in a concealing sweep—she had not thought about the situation with Oliver or Tam all morning!

'It's none of my business.'

'True,' he retorted in a cold, clipped voice that should not have made her feel hurt but did.

'What time do you plan on leaving?' As far as Miranda was concerned it couldn't be too soon!

'I already said I'm not.'

She was appalled. 'But you can't stay here… obviously.'

Gianni's dark brows lifted, emphasising the satyr-like slant she had previously noticed. *'No…?'* he drawled.

'It wouldn't be…appropriate.'

He watched her attempt to compress her lips and fail totally; her lush lips would not accommodate prim. 'How delightfully Victorian of you.'

Miranda refused to respond to the jibe.

'And I've always had a certain talent for the inappropriate.' His eyes drifted towards the soft outline of her spectacularly lush lips and any number of inappropriate actions occurred to him.

For a moment he could almost taste the sweetness and heat of her mouth as he slid his tongue deep… He pushed away the steamy images forming in his head, but not before the flash of testosterone-fuelled heat had settled painfully in his groin.

Dio, what was happening to him? He had left this sort of indiscriminate lust behind in his teens.

'How nice for you,' she said frigidly. 'But the fact remains that you'll have to leave.'

'Why?'

Was he trying to be obtuse? she wondered,

watching as Gianni unlatched the bottom of the stable door before stepping out into the yard, yelling, 'No, Liam, don't open the gate!' to his son, who was trying to gain access to the paddock with the duck pond.

'There's not enough room.'

He turned his head and angled a wry look tinged with amusement back at Miranda over his shoulder. 'Enough room? At last count there were five bedrooms.' Though two at least he could not stand upright in.

Ten bedrooms would not be enough to make her feel comfortable sharing a roof with this man. Her eyes drifted to the vee of golden skin at his throat. He was golden all over—things low in her belly flipped as she failed to block out the earthy image that had imprinted itself in her brain.

'Pity you didn't choose one of those last night,' she muttered under her breath as she slammed the fridge closed with unwanted force. She pitched her voice higher and added, 'I meant…' She paused, deciding it might not be such a good idea to say what she meant. Not even sure what she did mean…that he made her think inappropriate thoughts…?

'You came to see your…' she stopped, unable to bring herself to say aunt, finding the term too ludicrous to describe the relationship between the youthful and extremely gorgeous Lucy and this tall, rampantly Latin-looking man '…Lucy and she isn't here, so there's no need for you to stay.'

'Actually there's no need for you to stay,' he countered as he leaned a hand on the door jamb and glanced towards his son before returning his attention to Miranda. The wind blowing in ruffled his gleaming dark hair, making it stand up in tufts around his face. He smoothed it back with an impatient gesture.

'Don't worry, I'll make it right with Lucy.'

Miranda shook her head, bewildered by the promise. 'Make it…right?'

It wasn't until he reached into his pocket that she took his meaning.

'Has she paid you up front?' He extracted his hand empty… The lines around his eyes deepened as he tried to recall the last time he had seen his wallet.

A mixture of irritation and contempt on her face, Miranda lifted her chin. 'I don't want your money and I'm not going anywhere. I've been paid to do a job and I have every intention of fulfilling my contract.'

'I can look after the place for Lucy.'

Now that he considered the situation, Gianni could see there were advantages to Lucy being away. For starters he would not have to explain the situation to her—she never had made a secret of her disapproval for Sam, pronouncing herself unable to understand what motivated a woman who rejected her child, a woman who continued to risk her life doing the job she loved.

Gianni had tried to defend Sam, pointing out that Liam still had contact with his mother, she just left the hands-on parenting to him, but this cut no ice with Lucy.

'This is my job. I'm not here on holiday—I'm here to work. I can't walk away.'

'What—run a duster around the place and feed a few animals?'

The disparaging but essentially accurate description of her job brought a scowl to Miranda's brow.

'I think I can manage that.'

Miranda found herself wishing he could also manage to fall flat on his perfect face.

His dark eyes swept her face. 'I'm offering you a paid holiday here—who refuses an offer like that?'

Someone who didn't want to go home in time to see the newly-weds return, seeing the glow in Oliver's eyes when he looked at her sister.

'A kind offer, but I wouldn't dream of imposing. I'm being paid to do a job and I intend to do it.'

'Let's let Lucy decide. I think we'll find that she'd prefer family to be here.'

'Lucy rang yesterday when she landed—she's staying somewhere without a landline and there isn't a signal. She isn't due to check in again until next week—' Miranda broke off as a clucking hen ran through the kitchen door. Miranda clapped her hand, having more success in expelling this intruder. 'I'm not leaving...' She swallowed and heard the rising note of panic in her querulous addition, 'I can't!'

Gianni's brows lifted. So the redhead was running away...from what or who? Probably a love affair gone bad... It usually was, he thought cynically.

'I guess that means we'll have to cohabit.'

Miranda stared at him in horror, shaking her head at his idea of a solution. 'No...no, that's not possible. You can't stay. Why would you want to?' she challenged.

'For the pleasure of your charming company?'

Miranda gave a scornful snort and folded her arms across her chest, refusing to react to the charm.

'The fact is my work schedule doesn't allow... No, that's not true—I don't allow enough time to spend a lot of quality time with Liam.' Actually, he realised, this wasn't a lie. 'Quality time—I know it sounds corny, but it's true. I try, but not hard enough.' Again true.

He opened the door fully and stifled a pang of guilt. He couldn't afford to waver. When the circumstances necessitated you utilised your opponent's weaknesses and, for all her attitude, it was obvious that the redhead's weakness was a soft heart.

'Look at him,' he invited, gesturing towards Liam, who was playing with the dogs. 'He's having the time of his life. Sure, we could go back to London... But he'd be missing out—we both would.' He studied her from under the sweep of his lashes, watching while she struggled.

Miranda looked at the little boy playing outside. Gianni Fitzgerald's honesty had actually touched her. 'I'm not sure. I'd like to take you up on your offer, but...'

CHAPTER FIVE

THE dogs barking in the yard made Miranda break off mid sentence. She heard the sound of a car door slamming, then a male voice talking to the animals, who immediately quieted.

'Are you expecting visitors?' Sensing victory had been imminent, he cursed the timing of the interruption, now he had lost the advantage he had gained.

Miranda shook her head and got to her feet just as a man appeared framed in the top half of the stable door. His back turned to them, he rested the box he was carrying on the top of the closed section before turning.

'Sorry I'm late. I had some extra deliveries, but I put in some extra courgettes—we've got a glut—and Mum put in some of her elderflower cordial for you to try. She said thanks for the advice—the new hair cut—'

He saw them and stopped, an expression of

mild surprise spreading across his handsome face. 'Sorry, I didn't know Lucy had visitors…?'

She saw him look from her to Gianni to the child playing now at their feet before she could explain that this was not the cosy domestic scene it appeared at first glance—it felt important to disabuse him of any embarrassing misconception. Gianni spoke up.

'Lucy's away.'

The other man did not appear to pick up on the note of dismissal in Gianni Fitzgerald's voice that Miranda did.

'She is?'

'Yes.'

Gianni Fitzgerald, for all his smart tongue, could, it seemed, be a man of few words when it suited him; the rudeness was no major surprise.

'Perhaps she forgot to cancel her order?' Miranda suggested.

The newcomer gave a rueful shake of his head. 'Much more likely my brother forgot to tell me. He helps out on sufferance—he's more interested in getting back home to play his computer games.'

Miranda got to her feet and slid the latch holding the door. 'Do you want to put that on the table? It looks heavy.'

'Thanks.'

'I'm Miranda. I'm house-sitting for Lucy.'

'I'm Joe Chandler.' Young, blond and good-looking, Joe brushed his hand on his jeans before offering it to Miranda. She smiled at the sweet gesture and took it. 'Lucy takes one of our veggie boxes.'

'She did say something about it.'

'All organic.'

Gianni watched as the guy picked up a deformed-looking carrot from the top of the box and offered it for Miranda's inspection as if it were the Crown jewels.

'Lucy didn't say she was away—she always takes a box on Mondays and Fridays.'

Miranda took the muddy carrot, displaying the sort of interest his sisters might over a pair of designer shoes. 'Are they grown locally?'

If her interest was feigned, she was, Gianni decided, a very good actress.

'How much are the boxes?'

The guy mentioned an amount that seemed fairly extortionate for a few vegetables but Miranda appeared impressed.

'I'll take the usual,' she said cheerfully.

'That's great, but you'll probably need a bigger order with the family here?' he said with a glance towards Gianni.

'No, he's not with me, we're not…the regular order will be fine, thanks.' Her brow furrowed. 'How much do I owe you again?'

'I'll get that,' Gianni said, getting to his feet.

Miranda watched him frown as he began to search the pockets of the jacket slung over the arm of the kitchen chair and a switch suddenly clicked in her head.

Could she be guilty of missing the signs the way she had with her father?

The experience had made Miranda more sensitive to signs others might well have missed and she had already been puzzled by the contradictions: he wore expensive clothes, but drove a wreck of a car, but had driven, in Liam's words, a 'big, big car', now the 'lost' wallet—all suggested someone who had suffered a recent change of fortune...

Was it possible he wasn't being awkward for the sake of it but simply because he had nowhere else to go? Maybe like her father he had lost his job, possibly even his home. He wouldn't be the first man, as she knew only too well, who found the subject difficult to discuss.

Miranda made an impulsive decision. 'It's all right,' she said quietly. 'I've got it,' she added, extracting the notes from her purse, and handed them to Joe before she made a few more admiring noises about the contents.

'Shall I bring the usual delivery on Monday, then?'

'Yes, please, that would be lovely.' She followed Joe out into the yard discussing the next delivery.

Her thoughts very much on the man indoors and

his possible situation, it took her a moment to respond to Joe's surprise invitation.

'A drink in the pub?'

'About eight-thirty. I'm meeting a few friends. I could pick you up if you like…?'

On the point of refusing, she suddenly thought, *Why not?*

Back in the house she got straight to the point. 'Look, I've been thinking and you're right—there's plenty of room for us all here.' She reached for the coffee pot and filled her mug. 'In fact you'd be doing me a favour.'

Startled by this sudden turnaround, Gianni stared at her suspiciously.

'I would?'

'Yes…this place is a bit in the middle of nowhere, and I'd be nervous at nights here alone…'

Convinced he was missing something, but not sure what, Gianni put his hand over his mug before she ladled sugar into it. 'You do not strike me as the nervous type.'

Her eyes slid from his. 'Well, I am. Look, do you want to stay or not?'

His brow furrowed. 'I want to stay,' he admitted.

'Fine, well, I'm sure we can manage without getting in each other's way—it's a big house.' *Who are you trying to convince, Mirrie?* 'Look, I'll leave you to… I'll just go muck out the horses.'

It was delaying the inevitable but she spent the rest of the morning with the animals. At one point Liam joined her, wanting to ride on the donkey, but before she could respond his father appeared.

'Come on, Liam.'

'Oh, he's fine with me.' It was the father who she was anxious to avoid; the child was a joy.

Gianni took his son's hand. His eyes were inexplicably cold as they brushed her face. 'I don't need a babysitter. Liam is with me.'

Mirada watched him stride away, almost dragging the reluctant boy, fuming at his rudeness. What was his problem? The way he had acted you'd have thought she was about to steal the boy!

Well, as far as she was concerned he could go… well, go anywhere where she wasn't.

Having stretched her chores outside as far as lunchtime, she went indoors, but only to get her car keys. Lucy had mentioned the weekly farmer's market in the nearby town. Miranda had planned to visit it and the idea of escaping the house at the moment was an extra incentive to bring forward her plan.

There was no sign of her house guests, though she did not look too hard. Instead she left a note on the kitchen table explaining where she'd gone.

The market was every bit as good as Lucy had

said and she spent a few pleasant hours wandering around the colourful stalls.

It was after six by the time she returned to find the remains of a supper were on the kitchen table and there were sounds coming from the adjoining sitting room.

She dropped her bags, pulled out the sweets she had bought for Liam and went into the sitting room. For a few moments she stood unobserved in the doorway feeling a quiver in the region of her heart as she watched Liam, already in his pyjamas, shrieking with excitement, being chased around the room by his dad, who was on all fours pretending to be a bull.

When Liam saw her he ran to her, wrapping his arms around her legs in a hug in a gesture of childish spontaneity. 'Come play, let Daddy catch you, Mirrie!'

'Not just now, Liam,' Miranda said, glancing towards the older Fitzgerald, who was not looking so pleased to see her.

He dragged dark hair back from his broad brow with an impatient hand. 'Not now, Liam, go upstairs. It's bedtime.'

Miranda watched the little boy bounce from the room and held out the bag of sweets to Gianni. 'I thought he might like these? You know, he might go to sleep a little easier if—'

'I'm sure your knowledge of childcare is second to none, but I know Liam and he doesn't eat sweets.' He pushed them back at her, his fingers brushing her arm.

Miranda jumped as the light contact sent an electric surge through her body. Stepping backwards with a gasp, she knocked a half-full coffee cup off the dresser. She caught it but the contents tipped over her top.

His dark eyes brushed hers. The predatory gleam in the dark depths sent her stomach into a diving spin. His manner as cold as his eyes had been hot, Gianni made no comment as he left the room.

To the casual observer, she realised, the scene would be one of cosy domesticity: a woman washing up the supper dishes while the dogs played around her feet.

What the casual observer would not see was the general turmoil in her head. The 'cosiness' did not even go skin deep, she reflected, glancing at her forearm—it still tingled. She gave a shiver and plunged her hands deep into the hot water.

'Down!' None of the dogs responded to her half-hearted rebuke.

It was never going to work, she decided, wishing she had not given in to the spontaneous impulse that had made her agree to this crazy house share.

For all she knew her instincts might be totally off. It wasn't as if he came across as some sort of charity case.

Would she have been quite so keen to have him around if he hadn't been, on a scale of one to ten, a solid fifteen?

'No!' Miranda said, rejecting the idea with a firm shake of her head as she lifted her hands from the water and blew the suds from her pink fingers. 'I am not that shallow.'

But I am talking to myself.

It was true, though, and the knowledge that she had never been a person influenced or attracted by a pretty face made her feel moderately better about her motivation, if not the situation.

She closed her eyes and saw the gleam of raw male appreciation glittering in those dark depths and felt her stomach flip. She opened her eyes and thought, *I felt like a woman, a pretty woman.*

When was the last time that happened?

Did he manage to make every woman he met feel as if she were the only woman on the planet? If so it was quite a gift and the fact he had seemed to like what he saw when he looked at her had been soothing to someone whose ego had taken several rounds of bashing recently.

The memory of the hungry, predatory gleam she had seen in his eyes surfaced and before she could push it away a rash of goose bumps erupted on the surface of her suddenly too hot skin. She felt a flash of shame, guiltily aware that she was getting turned on by the thought of a man she didn't even like.

She wasn't even sure that her half-baked suspicions were true. She'd invented an entire tragic back story on the flimsiest of evidence... It wouldn't be the first time her soft heart—or soft head, according to her less gullible twin—had got her taken for a ride.

This could be like the time she had opened her purse to give the homeless guy with the sweet dog some change and been mugged, her purse and phone taken all over again. The homeless guy turned out not to be homeless and he'd stolen the dog.

Now it wasn't a dog, it was a cute kid. At least on this occasion the kid wasn't stolen. She glanced at her watch and frowned. *He's here and you'll just have to work with it, Mirrie,* she told herself, adopting a brisk expression as she folded the damp tea towel. Her expression morphed into annoyance as she registered the time. Another hour and Joe would be here. She glanced down at her soiled shirt, her lips moving in a moue of distaste. She needed to change and move her things, which were still in the bedroom adjoining Liam's.

Feeling an extreme reluctance to enter the room while Gianni was liable to walk in any moment,

she chewed the plump curve of her lower lip, wondering if she should clear out her stuff now or wait
until he had finished settling Liam.

How much longer was he going to be?

A bang on the ceiling above followed by the unmistakable sound of small running footsteps and
childish laughter overlaid by a deeper base tone
suggested that the answer was not any time soon.

She struggled to feel any sympathy for the
man who was having trouble persuading his son
it was time to go to bed. Even though she was not
normally a person who took pleasure from the
trials of others, Miranda did feel a small—all
right, quite large—stab of 'I told you so' satisfaction… Only she hadn't had the chance to tell him
anything—he had cut her off at the knees when
she had dared to offer advice.

When Miranda entered the bedroom she had used
the previous night a few minutes later, the laughter
had been replaced by sobs, so loud and inconsol-
able she gave a grimace of sympathy. Ashamed of
her previous spite, she even felt a flash of admiration. She couldn't hear what Gianni was saying,
but she was able to recognise the even-tempered
soothing quality in his deep voice.

She stood for a moment listening to the soft
rumble. There was no denying Gianni did have
a particularly attractive voice, deep accented and

smoky. She wondered if he'd ever thought of getting voice-over work. With his ability to make the most innocent of comments sound like an indecent proposal he'd never be short of work... *Or is that me hearing what I want to?*

The additional thought sent a sliver of shocked alarm through Miranda as she shook her head in a firm negative motion. The thought that she'd want a man like him to proposition her was laughable!

Because he's got nothing going for him beside a beautiful face, a perfect body and bucketloads of sex appeal.

She gave a tiny sigh of defeat... All right, she was not totally immune to his charms, when he chose to be charming, but he didn't always choose to be so. In fact he could be totally obnoxious!

An image of the bold bronzed features lingering stubbornly in her head, she tiptoed over to the wardrobe, her furtive technique more instinct than necessity. She could have blown a bugle and nobody would have heard her above the battle royal going on in the next room.

Flinging open the wardrobe door, she grabbed the first thing that came to hand. It happened to be the only skirt she had packed. Scrunching it carelessly into a ball, she dashed over to the big scrubbed pine chest. She slid open one of the big heavy drawers, wincing as it made a loud squeak-

ing sound, and snatched up the folded blouse that
lay on top.

Objective achieved, she made a breathless dash
to the bathroom where behind the locked door she
performed a lightning change. Peeling off her cof-
fee-soaked jeans and tee shirt, she stuffed them
with a grimace of distaste into the linen hamper.
Resisting the lure of the shower, she fought her
way into the clean clothes and glanced at herself
in the mirror.

Amazingly the things she had grabbed didn't
clash. The pale apple-green of the silky sleeveless
top with the loose cowl neck actually picked out a
contrasting darker green in the swirly pattern of
the long skirt that swished against her bare legs
as she moved.

Back in the bedroom Miranda worked quickly,
first sweeping all her cosmetics off the dressing
table into her open case before lugging it to the
bed and cramming everything from the drawers inside. Aware that things had gone very quiet
next door, she emptied the wardrobe, not both-
ering to remove anything from the hangers as,
casting frequent worried glances towards the connecting door, she piled them on top, responding
to the blind instinct that was telling her she had
to get out.

Miranda had no idea why logically the need
to vacate the room before Gianni reappeared had

taken on the form of something approaching compulsion, but it had and she didn't question it.

The way her luck was running today it was no real surprise that Gianni appeared in the doorway just as she was cramming the last of her possessions in her suitcase.

She could feel his eyes on her back but pretended not to be aware of his presence. She was though. Her skin prickled with it; the air in the room seemed charged with the sexual aura that he exuded. She had never met a man who was this overtly masculine.

Gianni, his thoughts on the brandy that Lucy kept in the dresser for emergencies—today definitely qualified—paused in the doorway when he saw Miranda.

As he pulled the door quietly to behind him she tucked a swag of vibrant hair behind her ears. Gianni's chest lifted in a silent sigh of appreciation as his heavy-lidded eyes moved to the swan-like curve of her pale neck; he was fascinated by the almost opalescent sheen of her satiny skin. He studied her profile, considering the extreme delicacy of her fine-boned, almost elfin features. Her jaw was rather firm, the pointed chin suggesting an obstinate nature.

Shifting his position slightly so that he could have a decent view of her full, soft mouth—a man who had just been through what he had deserved the odd treat—he leaned back against the door jamb, pressing a hand to the back of his neck when the muscles there cramped.

It struck him as ironic that a small child had been able to do what being put in the driving seat of a publishing empire had not. People frequently remarked on his stamina and ability to stay cool when those around him were in meltdown... If they could only see him now!

He could work thirty-six hours at a stretch in what most people would have considered a high-powered and stressful environment, but when he walked away he had never felt quite as exhausted as he did now, after spending sixty minutes trying to get a tired and extremely cranky four-year-old to sleep.

He glanced down at his watch. No, it had only been thirty minutes; it felt like a lot longer!

It had come as a nasty surprise, and didn't gel with his mental image of himself as a pretty clued-up, hands-on dad. He still couldn't figure out why his previously angelic son was acting out. On the previous occasions when he read his son his bed-time story—Gianni tried to make it home before his son went to bed at least three times a week—the little boy, already bathed and in his pyjamas, cuddled up and was invariably asleep before the third page.

Gianni felt his mood take an upward swing as

he noticed the gauzy skirt she had changed into and the way it clung to the slight but feminine curves of her bottom and thighs. She knew he was there but she was stubbornly ignoring him. Amusement moved at the backs of his dark eyes, mingling with the predatory gleam.

CHAPTER SIX

'ARE you sulking?'

Miranda's head turned sharply at the accusation, causing her hair to flick across her face. As he watched her push it away with an impatient hand Gianni remembered how it had looked spread out on the white pillow that morning.

Miranda's response to the charge was icily indignant. 'I do not sulk.' As their eyes connected she felt her indignation slip away.

He looked tired, she thought, noting the lines bracketing his sensually sculpted mouth. The gleam in his dark watchful eyes as they captured hers was not tired; it was hungry; it was…combustible… Miranda felt a stab of undiluted breath-robbing lust.

Bemused and deeply alarmed by the strength of her reaction, she turned her head sharply, allowing her hair to fall in a bright fiery shield around her flushed face as she tried to slow her rapid breathy inhalations.

'I'm busy.' She flashed him a dismissive look, taking care not to meet his eyes, and turned back to her task.

Gianni, long accustomed to women making the running, was astounded. It was one thing to decide regretfully to keep her at arm's length; it was another to be rebuffed.

'I suppose you heard that?' he drawled, tipping his head in the direction of the room he had just left.

'Hard not to,' Miranda said, trying to cram the lid on the case while studiedly ignoring the tingling feeling on the nape of her neck and the aching sensitivity of her breasts.

'I can't understand it. He usually goes out like a light…' he mused, his voice trailing away as his interest was captured by the seductive sway of her hips.

Nobody would have described her as voluptuous, but she was in her sleek way one of the most naturally feminine women he had ever met.

Miranda reached the limit of her tongue-biting and straightened up with a snap, the ringlets of her fiery hair settling with an energetic bounce around her shoulders.

'Is part of his bedtime routine normally a rough-and-tumble game that has him wound up tighter than a spring?'

His brow furrowed. 'Bedtime routine?'

Miranda was torn between amusement and disbelief at his bemused expression. 'A quiet time to help him wind down; milky drink, warm bath…' She arched a questioning brow and tilted back her head to look him in the face.

The furrow between his dark brows smoothed before it appeared again, only deeper, as now he was struck by the possibility that his model father status had more to do with the expert help he received than his own natural talent for parenting.

Not only did he have the services of a full-time nanny and a housekeeper who was always willing to lend a hand, but his mother took Liam most weekends. This practice began when Liam was a baby and had only ever been intended to be short term, but it had become something of a routine.

'Clare has normally done that stuff by the time I get in—'

'So Clare is your girlfriend? Sorry—it's none of my business.'

'That has never stopped any woman I know sticking her nose in. Clare is Liam's nanny. She's been with us since he was born.' His brow furrowed. 'I think he's missing her.'

And now he'd had to let the nanny go, along with his car and, for all she knew, his home. 'You've got the essentials right.' If parenting was, as she believed, about caring, Gianni Fitzgerald could not be faulted. 'The other things you can learn. I suppose this is all pretty new to you.'

He reacted with visible suspicion to her unthinking comment. 'Why would you suppose that?'

'Look, there's no need to pretend.'

On the receiving end of a look of warm, sympathetic understanding, not familiar ground for him, Gianni shook his head and struggled to stop his eyes straying to the plump swell of her small but perfectly formed breasts underneath the silky green top.

He put down his uncharacteristic lack of control to the long and trying day.

It had begun well, though. A reminiscent smile tugged at the corners of his lips as the memory of waking up next to her naked warm body took hold. He looked at her pink lips and thought about their tongues tangling, the heat and moisture, the taste... A stab of lust sent a lick of hungry heat through his body.

The silence stretched uncomfortably. Miranda read the tension in his taut, edgy expression. 'I shouldn't have said anything,' she admitted remorsefully.

Gianni hardly heard. 'You look nice,' the man famed for his charm and smooth lines with the opposite sex heard himself say.

Nice...? Had he been taken over by an alien life form? 'Very...' his eyes made a sweep of her supple curves before he swallowed and added with a nod in the direction of her skirt '…feminine.'

Miranda saw through this supposed interest in her outfit. 'You don't have to change the subject.'

'I didn't know I was.' Making a fool of himself was another matter; on that score, he thought irritably, he had no doubts at all.

His jaw tightened as he considered his behaviour. He had not struggled to think above waist level since he was a teenager, but for some reason he was unable to look at this woman without thinking of her minus clothes. This was a long way from the harmless appreciation of an attractive woman's shape. Given he was a mature, moderately intelligent male able to control his appetites, he could only assume that his continuing fixation was connected with their extremely unconventional meeting.

It wasn't a mystery: he'd seen her naked and he wanted to again.

'I understand. I really do.' She lowered her gaze and looked up at him through the mesh of her lashes. 'My dad lost his job two years ago.'

His dark eyes narrowed fractionally at this seemingly disconnected piece of information and he allowed himself a cautious, 'Sorry.' He tipped his dark head and wondered where this was going. It crossed his mind that she might see him as some sort of potential employer for her father…but realised almost immediately that didn't work unless she knew who he was…

'He was so ashamed that he didn't tell a soul.' A shadow crossed her face. It was still hard to speak about a time that had been really hard for the family. 'It was as if his self-esteem was wrapped in what he did. When he lost his job I think he kind of lost his identity…'

Not quite sure how to respond to this additional information, and wondering about the entire hidden-message thing she had going on, Gianni gave a non-committal grunt.

'We didn't have a clue. He got up every morning and put on his suit, kissed my mum goodbye and went, or so we all thought, to work as normal.'

Gianni felt a stab of sympathy for the man he had never met. 'What did he do?'

'He actually went to the library. Of course, it wasn't quite the same for him. He was nearly pensionable age. It was not so much about loss of income as he felt he'd been put on the scrap heap. I suppose if something like that happens when you're younger,' she said, fixing him with a steady look, 'and used to having…nice things, it must be hard to…readjust. But there's no shame in being unemployed. You just have to remember it's only temporary and children don't care what car you drive—they care about the love and attention they receive.'

It took a few seconds for Gianni to realise that this earnest little morality tale was aimed at him. She actually thought she was talking about him. His incredulity gave way to annoyance that almost immediately tipped over into amusement.

The question of why she had suddenly thought it was a good idea for him to stay was solved—he was a charity case.

'And you're bound to make a few mistakes at first but look at all the things you're doing right.'

'There are things I am doing right?' Coming clean was the right thing to do, but not the most convenient thing to do.

'Well, you didn't lose your temper when he was playing up. A lot of people would.'

'What are you doing?' he asked, watching as she pressed her knee into the bulging case on the bed.

Perhaps, Gianni reflected, it was a question best directed to himself.

What was he doing?

He had a healthy libido, but he also had the ability to compartmentalise his life. The fact was he could not remember the last time he'd had such a strong physical reaction to a woman, though even had the circumstances been different he doubted he would have acted on the attraction. While he was not looking for a soul mate—if such a thing existed—in his bed, neither was he looking for the sort of challenge Miranda would provide.

Gianni saved his energy for boardroom fights; in bed he preferred something involving less effort emotionally. But anyway it was all academic. She knew Liam; that put her off limits romantically speaking. After the Laura incident he made damn sure that his lovers and his son had no contact. It was the one unbreakable rule... The question was, would it be so bad to bend it a little... temporarily?

His lips twisted into a grimace as he reminded himself of the mistakes he'd made in his first relationship as a single father——the first had been letting it last too long, the second had been letting his tiny son become attached to Laura.

It had not even crossed Gianni's mind to consider the potential impact having a girlfriend might have on his son. At the time he'd still been adjusting to his role as a single parent and proving himself in his new job at the time, as a political editor for a broadsheet. On both counts it had been a steep learning curve. Being embedded with the military in a war zone had been a stroll in the park by comparison. A high-maintenance girlfriend was the last thing he had needed, but he had also recognised he wasn't equipped to live the life of a monk. Though there had been occasions since then he had wondered if the short-lived affair had been less about satisfying his sexual desires and more about a need to prove to himself

that he was over Sam, while at the same time rid-
ding himself of any lingering concern that making a total fool of yourself or standing there with
a sign saying 'rip out my heart then stamp on it'
were habit forming.

It turned out they weren't. At no time during
the enjoyable interlude with Laura had he felt a
return of the crazy compulsion to declare his un-
dying love. But then neither had he begun a day
by having his life saved by a helmet that took a
bullet intended for his skull.

In the euphoria that had followed this brush with
death he had decided that life was too damned
short. Why waste time on the formalities, the polite conventions of courtship, when it was obvious that he and Sam were meant to be together—it
was inevitable.

So, bottle of champagne in his hand, a lurid
bruise beginning to develop on his forehead, spent
bullet in his camouflage jacket pocket and not a
thought of rejection in his head, Gianni had proposed to the woman he had been convinced was
his soul mate only to have her look deeply embarrassed.

Sam's admission that she wasn't looking for a
relationship, let alone marriage—but the sex had
been good—had not been intentionally cruel, but
Gianni, who for the first time in his life had imagined himself in love, had still felt as though some-

one had kicked him hard in his most vulnerable region.

Having experienced it once, only a fool would invite that sort of pain and humiliation again, so instead of looking for love he had invited Laura into his bed and it had been a mutually enjoyable interlude.

When they were together he had enjoyed the sex and when they were not together he had not thought about her—perfect. The end of the arrangement a few months later when Laura had started dating a senior partner in the law firm where she worked had not left him bitter and twisted. He had not felt slighted when Laura had said she would miss Liam and not him. It was only when it became clear that Liam was missing the pretty woman who had entered his life and then left that he realised how selfish he had been.

The solution was to his mind obvious: in future he would keep his lovers and his son separate. Some women didn't like the boundaries he set, but no woman was to his mind indispensable— but this one was very desirable, he conceded as his hooded gaze slipped back to Miranda's bottom before lifting to the outline of her small plump breasts.

An image of her lying in the bed beside him formed in Gianni's head; the warm scent of her body, the smooth, satiny skin. He found his firm resolve wavering… It would make being holed up here a lot less painful if he could find oblivion from the problems in his life in her soft body.

Miranda turned her head and caught a look of raw male appreciation in the dark eyes trained on her.

With no warning a blast of heat flowed through her body as she stood frozen like a feral creature caught in the headlights.

A silence hummed in the still air as they stood, glances locked. Even the breeze, it seemed to her, had stopped blowing through the open window. The room was hot and heavy and every breath she drew was an effort.

She had never considered herself any man's idea of an erotic fantasy and she had never minded telling herself she would much prefer to be appreciated for her personality and mind. She might have to rethink that, she decided as she turned away, her body still gently thrumming with sexual awareness. There were decided plus points to being looked at like a sex object.

'What does it look like? I'm moving to another room.' The barn was suddenly looking like not a bad option either.

Gianni shook his dark head and protested. 'I can't chuck you out of your room, *cara*.'

The casual Latin endearment made the hairs on her nape prickle. 'It makes sense for me to move,' she retorted, thinking especially when the option was Gianni Fitzgerald going through her room at all hours to get to his son.

'You need to be close to Liam.'

Gianni conceded the practical point with a shrug.

'And I would appreciate a little privacy. It's bad enough sharing the house with you without sharing—' She stopped mid sentence, feeling the gauche flush rise to her cheeks, and added gruffly, 'Everything.'

One dark brow moved in the direction of his hairline as he glanced towards the neatly made bed. 'Don't worry—the next time I'll wait until I'm invited.'

The soft suggestive drawl caused her stomach muscles to take an unscheduled dive. She straightened briefly from her task and met his gaze, amazed that she could appear so calm when her heart was racing fast enough to set off cardiac monitors in the next county.

'You'll have a long wait.'

The lines around his eyes deepened attractively as his glance dropped with slow deliberation to her mouth. 'A challenge?'

She lifted her chin. 'A fact.'

'Some things are worth waiting for.' He repeated the well-known maxim and wondered if that was where he had been going wrong. Everything in his life came easily except for being a father, maintaining a good relationship with his son's mother, sustaining a healthy work-home balance and... Actually, he realised, nothing in his life came easy except sex.

His eyes trained on her soft mouth. It seemed a good juncture to remind himself that the last thing he needed was sex with a redhead who thought he was some sort of charity case, basically a homeless, jobless no-hoper.

Miranda directed a frustrated glare at his golden-toned perfect profile. The man wouldn't recognise rejection if it bit him. 'Not me,' she blurted without thinking.

'Let me be the judge of that.' *Except you're not going to, Gianni. You sleep with women guaranteed to run at the first hint of financial ruin.*

'It's true,' she began, then stopped, realising with horror that she'd been pushed to the brink of explaining to him that she simply didn't have a passionate nature. She was actually surprised that a man who was clearly not exactly inexperienced with women had not picked up on that immediately.

Oliver obviously had, and he wasn't by any stretch of the imagination what you could call a ladies' man. Or maybe, she speculated, it wasn't so much what she gave off but what she didn't. Oliver had talked to her almost every day for two years and then along had come Tam with her identical face and very similar body and Oliver had been totally smitten.

Miranda's chest lifted in a sad, silent sigh as she considered the mystery that was sexual attraction. Whatever it was, it wasn't about looks alone. Of course, some people had both. She angled a resentful look at Gianni Fitzgerald's face. He had the looks and then some. Their eyes connected and Miranda felt a flash of heat run through her body. Trying hard to ignore the places the heat pooled and lingered, she lifted her chin.

'I'm not going to let you be anything!' she exclaimed, then glancing to the connecting door and lowering her voice as she added, 'Look, I can see that you can't help flirting with anything with a pulse, but I'm here to do a job, not bolster your ego or be a...a...television substitute.'

The fierce addition drew a startled rumble of laughter from Gianni's chest. 'I can honestly say that I have never thought of you in those terms. Aren't you afraid that you'll injure my already damaged fragile male ego with a rejection?' Without waiting for a reply, he bent towards her open case and shook his head. 'You know, it might have helped if you'd taken them off the hangers. You know what they say—more haste, less speed. Do you want a hand there?'

Miranda squared her shoulders, uncomfortably

aware of the trickle of moisture tracing a sticky path between her shoulder blades.

'I've got things under control.' Aware the statement was untrue on more levels than she wanted to analyse, she added a stiff polite, 'Thank you.'

If she was going to spend what was as yet an unspecified amount of time under the same roof as this provocative man she had to do something about the uncomfortable degree of self-consciousness she felt around him.

She had to relax.

Easier said than done when she felt tense and edgy just thinking about his dark eyes when they were fixed on her, one moment icy and aloof, the next gleaming in a way that suggested he was enjoying some private joke at her expense. She wanted to— She closed her eyes for a split second to compose herself and shook her head, annoyed with herself for wasting time and energy in trying to analyse the way he made her feel.

Letting him get under her skin wasn't helping.

Bottom line—he was annoying; she didn't like him. He was also wildly attractive and sexy and, boy, did he know it!

To make this experience as painless as possible she had to chill out. There was no point being openly antagonistic, especially as she had the impression he liked getting a rise out of her. How hard could it be?

She had loved Oliver and she had been able to control her actions and feelings around him; she had no feelings beyond irritation for Gianni Fitzgerald.

'I feel bad making you move.'

'You're not making me do anything,' she retorted, transferring her anger to the zip, which moved an inch before the overstressed teeth parted company and her clothes spilled out onto the bed in a tumble of textures and colour.

Miranda swore through gritted teeth.

'Not a word I particularly want to add to Liam's vocabulary.'

The dry rebuke brought a sting of hot embarrassment to her cheeks. 'Sorry. I don't normally—' She stopped and bit her lip, aware that she was apologising a lot.

Gianni watched her through his thick dark lashes, a smile playing around his lips, watching her ineffectual efforts to gather the clothes. She was easy to watch; there was, he decided, something almost feline about the way she moved.

She angled an antagonistic glare over her shoulder. 'What are you looking at?'

'You. Let me!'

About to protest, Miranda, who had dropped to her knees beside the bed, stopped herself, and instead shrugged and sat back on her heels.

'Feel free,' she said, waving her arm in a gesture of irritable invitation.

She stood there and watched while he separated the large items she had left on hangers, shook them and draped them across her arm.

'You all right with those?'

'I'm fine.'

Stomping up the stairs, trying to peer over the top of the clothes, she could hear him coming up behind her. When she reached the bedroom door she paused and, disentangling one hand from the clothes folded over her arms, reached for the handle. Nudging the door with her hip, she stepped inside.

'This is a lovely room.' And, more importantly, an entire floor away from him.

'It's a cupboard,' he contradicted, stepping in after her and causing the modestly sized room to contract even more with, not just his physical size, but his overpoweringly masculine presence.

She watched through her lashes, feeling the heat rise inside her as he bent and placed her case on the bed, pressing it with his hand as he did so. He really did have the sort of physique that any athlete would envy.

Caught in the act of ogling—yes, there was no other word for what she was doing, she acknowledged shamefully—Miranda felt her face turn a shamed pink.

He arched a questioning brow and produced a lopsided sardonic smile that was sinfully attractive. Despite the smile his eyes glowed with something that had nothing to do with amusement, the expression in the dark depth, causing her stomach muscles to quiver frantically.

Miranda lifted her chin. 'What?' she snapped belligerently.

'This bed is like a rock.'

Miranda blinked. 'I like a firm mattress,' she contended.

'I'm curious—if I say black, will you say white?'

Miranda rolled her eyes.

'And while we're talking reverse psychology...'

'We're not talking reverse anything. You're talking rubbish.'

'If I say don't kiss me, will you?'

CHAPTER SEVEN

MIRANDA glared at Gianni, opened her mouth to say, *In your dreams*, and found herself instead grabbing his shirt and pulling herself up on tiptoe to press her lips to his.

For a moment he did nothing, then just as she was pulling away he returned the pressure, his lips moving with sensuous skill that made Miranda, who was conscious of the unleashed power in him, tremble.

She was still trembling when he put her away from him, physically depositing her a few feet away before taking an extra step back. *As though*, she thought as she swallowed the hysterical laughter in her throat, *I might leap at him again*.

'I don't know why I did that.' The embarrassment she felt was so oppressive she could hardly look at him.

He did and he was ashamed that he had instigated it. 'This situation is awkward. I'm not used to—'

Not used to having his son and a woman he had

wanted to sleep with under the same roof. His eyes slid to the delicious curve of her wilful mouth and he swallowed, unable to control the response of his body.

'I keep my personal life and Liam totally separate.' It had never been a problem previously. 'No exceptions. It's a…a…'

'Rule?'

The Fitzgeralds, it seemed, were big on rules, though Lucy, with her lists, had stopped short of regulating Miranda's sex life. It was not a subject that up to this point had needed regulation. Miranda had never been a very sensual person and she was not sorry about it; she had seen where giving in to sexual impulses got a person.

'Yes, if you like. Liam is the only permanent thing in my life.' The women, they came and went.

The warning was not exactly subtle— *Don't go getting any ideas.* It was a message she realised he'd been sending all day. But, my God, had his messages been mixed, she thought, recalling with indignation all the hot and cold looks he'd been dishing out.

She adopted an expression of mock dismay and batted her eyelashes Bambi-style.

'Does that mean we're not getting married?'

His smile flickered. 'You're angry?'

She widened her eyes in a show of shocked admiration. 'My God, you're psychic!'

'Look, don't take this personally. In other circumstances I...' As he held her eyes Miranda felt
the air thicken. 'You're an attractive woman.'

'And you're not nearly so irresistible as you
think you are.'

'You kissed me,' he was pushed to retort.

'And you make casual, shallow sex seem some
sort of noble sacrifice rather than an inability to
form any sort of relationship with a woman.

'I happen to know someone who wasted eight
years of her life on someone who couldn't com-
mit. He didn't have a son to blame for his insecu-
rities. He'd cheat, she'd leave and then he'd come
crawling back with some rubbish excuse and she
finally woke up.'

The talk of the friend who had repeatedly gone
back to a cheating boyfriend did not fool him; nobody displayed that sort of emotion about a friend,
no matter how close. Miranda had been talking
about herself.

She walked to the door and pushed it wide.
'Look, if you don't mind, Joe will be here in a
minute.'

'Joe who?'

'Joe Chandler.'

'Is that meant to mean something to me?'

'The veggie-box man—you met him earlier.
He asked me to go for a drink with him.' Gianni
Fitzgerald might be able to resist her, but it was

good to be able to show him not everyone was so damned picky!

Gianni paused and watched her walk through the open door, then turned back, refusing to recognise the emotion he was battling to control as jealousy. He was not a jealous man.

'And you said yes?'

'I don't see how that's any of your business, but as a matter of fact I did.'

Annoyance flashed across his face. 'Is that wise?'

Miranda stared, totally stunned by his censorious attitude and then, as she thought about it, angry. 'Wise?' she echoed, thinking, *Not wise was kissing you. What the hell were you thinking of, Mirrie?* 'I thought I'd throw caution to the winds.'

'And go out with a total stranger?'

'You're a total stranger, and what are you talking about? Joe is a perfectly nice man. Not to mention,' she added with a small reflective smile, 'rather attractive.'

A muscle clenched in his jaw as he fought a violent wave of gut-clenching repugnance. 'You got dressed up for him?' *Who's she meant to get dressed up for, Gianni?* mocked the voice in his head.

'Yes,' she responded rather too belligerently.

'I know there's a school of thought that says

get right back on the horse when you fall off, but sometimes it's better to let the bruises heal.'

'The thing about analogies,' Miranda mused, getting angrier by the second, 'is they only work if the person you're talking to has the faintest idea what you're talking about.'

'You're obviously coming out of an unhappy relationship.'

She stared at him in utter astonishment. This man's arrogance was staggering. 'Before you go any further I should say I don't take advice on my love life—' or what passed for it '—from total strangers.'

'You just go out to dinner with them.'

'Not dinner, a drink, and I happen to be a very good judge of character.'

Miranda had no hesitation in refusing the offer of a taxi from a sheepish Joe, who'd had, as he readily admitted, 'one too many' to get behind the wheel of his car. The cottage was less than a mile away and she anticipated enjoying the walk back.

She did. It was really relaxing walking along quiet moonlit lanes, letting her mind go blank.

Her mellow mood dispersed a little as the cottage gate came in sight. With luck Gianni would be in bed and asleep. She didn't want another run-in with the wretched man to ruin what had been a really relaxing evening. Joe and the friends who had joined them had been relaxing and undemanding company.

The same could not be said of her housemate.

She felt the tension slide from her shoulders when she saw the house was in darkness—she was in luck. Letting herself quietly in through the back door, she murmured a soft, 'Hi, boys,' to the dogs, who lay in their baskets thumping their tails in sleepy greeting but not getting up.

Slipping off her shoes, she headed for the hall door. She was halfway across the room when the door of the massive fridge that sat in one corner of the room swung open, the light acting like a spotlight for that corner, illuminating, not just the fridge contents, but the man who stood in front of it with a bluish light.

Miranda released a scream then, riveted to the spot, stared at the man standing there. Gianni was wearing a pair of boxer shorts cut low on his narrow hips and nothing else.

She lifted a hand to her neck, covering the vulnerable area where a pulse was banging away frantically. Dear God, what did this man have against clothes?

'What sort of time do you call this?' Wasn't that what a worried parent or a jealous lover would say when he'd been pacing the floor glancing at the clock for the last two hours?

'Hilarious,' she gasped, letting her head fall for-

ward as she panted, waiting for her heart rate to
slow. This might have happened sooner than it
did had she not been tempted to peek through the
skeins of hair that hung around her face at the man
standing there.

He had the most incredible body!

There wasn't an ounce of spare flesh on his
lean, rangy frame to disguise the ridges of muscular definition on his flat belly or the utterly perfect
muscle formation of his chest and shoulders. His
legs were long, the hair-roughened thighs powerfully muscled—it was the sort of body a light
heavyweight might work years to achieve and then
fall short of this sort of athletic ideal.

God, no wonder he was arrogant. He was gorgeous and he had to know it!

Gianni listened to the audible sound of her la-
boured breathing and let out a long silent whistle. '*Dio*, but you're jumpy, woman… They say a
guilty conscience does that to a person. What have
you been up to, *cara*?'

The sly insinuation brought her head up with a
jerk. Smoothing her hair away from her flushed
face, she angled an unfriendly glare at him.

'What the hell are you doing lurking in the dark
like that? You nearly gave me a heart attack!'

'Me…?' He adopted an attitude of mock inno-
cence. 'I'm just getting a glass of milk,' he said,
raising the carton to his lips.

She watched as he proceeded to gulp down half the contents before he wiped his mouth with the back of his hand and slid the carton back inside the fridge.

'That is disgusting. Have you never heard of glasses or clothes?'

His brows lifted at the addition. 'Your night seems to have left you a little bit...tetchy. Did country boy not live up to expectations?' he drawled.

Her eyes narrowed. 'I had a lovely evening, thank you for asking—right up to the moment I walked in and saw you.'

His brows lifted. 'So he didn't.'

A sound of hissing frustration issued between her clenched teeth. 'Goodnight.'

'You know, I really don't think it's polite to leave a lady looking so...unfulfilled.'

In the act of turning away, she swung back. 'I'm totally fulfilled, thank you very much!'

His brows lifted at the spitting vehemence of her delivery. 'Glad to hear it. So lover boy is not coming in...didn't even walk you to the door...' He glanced towards the door and observed with a frown, 'I didn't hear a car...'

'Why—were you listening out for it? As a matter of fact I walked back.'

'He walked you home under the stars—a nice romantic touch.'

'God, you're one sarcastic—' She clamped her teeth over the insult hovering on her tongue. 'As a matter of fact I walked home alone.'

The mocking laconic pose disintegrated as he suddenly straightened up, looking dauntingly tall and forbidding. 'He let you walk home alone?' He closed his eyes and swore at length in his mother tongue.

'It's only half a mile!' she protested, thrown off balance by the lightning change in his attitude.

'Half a mile along isolated country roads with no street lights. A motorist would never have seen you, let alone avoided you, in that get-up,' he said, nodding towards the black coat she had worn over her skirt and top.

'There was no traffic,' she protested weakly.

He arched a brow. 'And you knew there wouldn't be, did you?'

His anger seemed inexplicable to Miranda, but there was no doubt that it was genuine. 'No, but—'

'And of course you knew for sure that there were no gangs of drunk, drug-crazed thugs who would have been only too happy to while away the odd hour with a lone female who looks like you! And we won't even bring homicidal maniacs into this discussion…'

Miranda blinked. He made it sound as though she'd strolled home through some inner-city red-light district in a miniskirt. 'The only thing I saw was a cat. I was perfectly safe. This is the country.'

'And only nice things happen in the country?'

'No, but—'

'Grow up, Miranda. He shouldn't have let you walk home alone.' His anger slipped away as his glance moved over the graceful curves of her body. The lust that replaced it was equally hard to control.

'I'm not afraid of the dark and you're scaring me more than anything I saw during my walk back.'

'I?' Gianni studied her face and looked quite shaken as he husked, 'I had no intention of scaring you.'

'No, just making me see bogey men in every shadow. I can see now that I should at least have worn something light, but I wasn't planning on walking back until Joe—'

'Got drunk?' Gianni shook his head, his hands hanging loosely at his sides balling into fists. 'What a loser!' he exclaimed in disgust.

Miranda felt impelled to defend the absent Joe. 'He's a perfectly nice man.'

'Who can't hold his booze and doesn't know what to do with a woman.' Gianni fought to contain the explosive anger building up inside him, not sure whom he was angrier with: himself for feeling jealous of such a man, or Miranda, who

was responsible for making him feel this way...
Dio, what was this woman doing to him?

She lifted her chin. 'And you do, I suppose?'
The scorn died from her eyes the moment they
made direct contact with his.

The tension in the room suddenly went through
the roof, along with Miranda's pulse rate.

'Try me, *cara*,' he drawled. 'I've not had any
complaints yet.'

Miranda aimed for a cool cutting tone but
missed by a mile. 'I'll pass, I don't do casual sex
with narcissistic men who spend their lives admiring themselves in the mirror.'

'I'm not the one looking, Miranda, you are, and
I'm getting the impression you like what you see.'

'You're disgusting!' she choked.

'I can be,' he agreed with a wicked grin. 'If
that's what you like?'

The soft insidious addendum sent a flash of heat
sizzling along her nerve endings. 'I like...I like...
not you!' she finished childishly. 'What are you
doing?' she asked, her voice sinking to a fearful
husky whisper as he began to stalk towards her
looking like the predator he undoubtedly was. The
knowledge should have disgusted her but instead
of revulsion it was excitement that unfurled deep
in her belly as she watched him move closer, his
casual attitude not hiding his determination.

He was a couple of feet away from her when the

fridge door swung closed of its own momentum, plunging the room into darkness, the gloom alleviated only by the moonlight shining through the chinks under the blinds.

She was struggling to adjust to the dim light when she heard his voice, deep and rich as dark chocolate, sinfully suggestive, come out of the darkness. 'Just as well you're not afraid of the dark, *cara*. You can look after me.'

'I'd prefer to look after a snake,' she countered with shaky defiance.

His laughter was closer than it had been, then as her eyes grew accustomed to the gloom she saw the outline of his body. He was so close, all she had to do was reach out and she could have touched him.

Shocked by how badly she wanted to do just that, Miranda tucked her hands behind her back and shook her head in bewilderment. She had never felt more scared or more excited in her life. The sexual awareness that she had always been conscious of around this man but had tried to ignore could no longer be ignored.

'Let me look after you, Miranda. I'll chase away the bogey men.'

'You are the bogey man.'

She heard his soft laugh, then felt his hand on her cheek. She flinched, but did not move away as he traced a path down her cheek and left his finger there by her mouth.

He was offering her sex.

Even more shocking than this was the discovery that she was tempted. He was so gorgeous and where was the harm? He wanted nothing from her, but her body was sending some unmistakable signals that it wanted what he was offering.

Why intellectualise this?

Why pretend the fact he had 'dominant male' stamped through him like a stick of rock didn't turn her on? She wasn't looking for a life partner, a soul mate; to put it crudely—and for once she did—she wanted sex.

There was no shame in acknowledging she had needs that, after years of lying dormant, had chosen to surface big time.

Hadn't that always been her problem? She thought too much.

She had spent years living a nunlike existence, saving herself for Oliver, and now here was a man offering her what she'd been missing out on—no strings.

She might not be able to have love, but that didn't mean she couldn't have pleasure, and if she was going to choose someone who knew how to give pleasure—if Gianni was half as good as he thought he was—it would be difficult to find someone more qualified.

'What about your rule?'

'Rules are made to be broken.'

'I don't have casual sex with strangers.' She made the statement as much for her own benefit as his.

'Then tell me to go away and I will.'

The silence stretched while Miranda struggled to think through the haze of desire in her head… Then she gave up fighting.

'I…I can't,' she admitted in a throaty whisper. 'I don't want you to go away.'

He was so close now she felt the sigh of his warm breath as it left his lips. Her nostrils flared as she breathed in the musky male scent of his warm body. He was so close now she was panting… Oh, God, panting!

What had happened to her?

She shook her head and thought, *I don't know or care but I'm damned well going to enjoy it.*

'Then I won't.'

Gianni lowered his head and in the darkness found her lips. They were soft and trembling. Without encouragement they parted and with a groan he deepened the kiss. Miranda met his tongue with her own in an instinctively sensuous stabbing movement.

The intimate exploration was so overwhelming she struggled to cling to any sense of self. She could feel and taste him everywhere. Then with a sigh she stopped trying and impossibly it felt even better.

Her body felt soft and pliant as he dragged her up hard against him, reaching with one hand to the neck of her top and sliding his hand down over one smooth, high breast, pushing his fingers under the thin lacy covering of her bra to find her nipple hard and erect.

She gasped, a quiver running through her body as he ran his thumb across the tight bud.

Gianni bent his head, pushing her hair away and whispering in her ear. 'You like that?'

'Yes, don't stop…' She reached up to touch his skin. It felt scalding hot and damp as she spread her fingers and moved her hands up over his ridged stomach towards his chest.

He tangled his fingers in her curls and dragged her face up to his. 'I won't.' He couldn't. There was a fever in his blood that Gianni had never in his life experienced. Her hands on the bare skin of his chest left trails of fire.

'Your skin feels incredible,' she said, her throaty voice raw with wonder. He was hard, his skin the texture of warm satin. 'You feel—oh, God!' she moaned, unable to press herself close enough. 'So good.'

He pressed a kiss to the base of her throat, pushing her slightly away. Her protest died as his fingers tugged at the buttons of her blouse, clumsy in his urgency to expose her body.

Their fingers touched as she tried to assist him. He murmured encouragement against her mouth as he continued to kiss her with a bruising intensity.

A frantic moment later her shirt was gone, flung over his shoulders; her bra quickly followed. She immediately stepped into him, raising herself up on her toes to draw his head down to her, crushing her breasts up flat against him and crying out as he pressed his erection hard against her pelvis.

They were still kissing when he picked her up and carried her from the darkened room as though she weighed nothing.

He carried her, not to the room next to Liam's, but up the next flight to her room in the eaves. Still kissing her, he walked backwards through the door into the tiny bedroom.

Miranda had left the window open and not closed the curtains before she left and the room was filled with moonlight and the smell of the night-scented stock that drifted in on the night breeze that felt cool against her overheated skin.

She opened her eyes as he laid her on the bed. The sight of the big man who knelt over her sent a heavy pulse of languid longing through her body.

A tiny sob escaped her lips.

His hooded eyes flared, the darkness igniting

into flame as they swept over her body. Before his eyes locked on to hers she lay there breathing hard as he unfastened the belt on her skirt. He slid down the zip, bending to kiss the tiny indent above her belly button before he slid the skirt down over her hips.

A moment later her silky pants followed.

His eyes hadn't left hers for a moment. They did now, and the almost feral growl of appreciation that vibrated in his throat as he looked down at her naked body sent a pulse of lust slamming through her so intense that for a moment she struggled to catch her breath.

She closed her eyes. What was happening was so far out of her comfort zone she couldn't anticipate what her body would do next. She could feel what little control she had slipping away.

When she prised her heavy lids open she discovered he had removed his shorts. She sucked in a shocked breath, excitement zigzagged through her body like fork lightning and she felt an immediate flood of hot moisture pool between her thighs in reaction to the sight of his magnificently aroused body.

'If you carry on looking at me like that, *cara*, this thing will be over before it is started,' he rasped throatily.

'S...sorry.' He was watching her and not moving. His stillness had an explosive quality. The muscles in her stomach quivered violently; her mouth was dry.

'No apology required.'

She shivered and cried out as his hand curved over one breast, then his head was there, dark against her skin as he began to run his tongue over her aching flesh, moving closer to the tight, burning nipple before he finally took it into his mouth.

While he tasted her, his hands began to move, stroking and caressing her everywhere until her entire body was shaking and her skin was burning.

Then his tongue moved lower, the sensual exploration following his hands down her body. She jerked at the touch of his fingers along her inner thigh as he dragged her legs apart, causing her to gasp as he stroked the throbbing core of her pleasure. After the first shock she found herself moving with him, her hips rotating in time with the rhythmic caresses as she felt the pleasure build.

She gave a bewildered cry of protest when he moved away without warning.

'Hold that thought, *cara*.'

'What are you doing?'

'We need protection. I know, I know, sorry, but I promise I'll be back before you can say—'

'I want you,' she completed, her dissent giving way to anticipation at his explanation.

Gianni broke all records racing to his room and then back up. Sitting on the side of the bed, he removed the foil from the condom, stopping when he felt her hand curl around the smooth shaft of his erection.

The touch snapped his fragile control and with a growl he tipped her back on the bed. Sliding on the condom with one hand, he knelt between her pale thighs. Kissing her throat, he trailed his damp kisses towards her mouth as Miranda guided him with a shaking hand into her, her overpowering need overcoming doubt.

His astonished gasp was louder than Miranda's.

'Relax, *cara*, let's do this slow and sweet,' he crooned in her ear. 'You ready for this?'

'Please,' she whispered, grabbing his shoulders, feeling as though his beautiful voice was the one thing anchoring her to reality.

He began to move, stroking a hand down her flank as he looked down into her face, struggling for control as her tight, wet heat surrounded him, and gripped him, sucking him into her body deeper and deeper.

She could not believe the pleasure singing through her body. Every move he made produced new and wonderful mind-numbing sensations. 'You feel…oh, Gianni, you're so good at this… very, very, very good—do you know that?'

Miranda moved with him, breathless, clinging, every fibre of her body straining for release…up to the point where she really thought she'd lose consciousness. Then when it came the release was like a starburst, wave after wave of intense thrumming pleasure that hummed through her entire body.

CHAPTER EIGHT

GIANNI still lay on top of her breathing hard when she said, 'I'd really like to do that again.'

Miranda felt the laughter in his chest before he grunted and rolled off her. 'I pride myself on my quick recovery time, but give a man a second to catch his breath.'

They lay side by side, breathing hard, the sweat on their skins cooling until Miranda started laughing.

He turned his head at the soft sound and murmured drily, 'Not a reaction I have ever had before.' Luckily his ego was fairly sturdy or he might be feeling worried instead of just…exhausted. His eyes slid down her supine body. Her smooth skin glistened pearly pale beneath a fine layer of sweat, her pink-tipped little breasts still bore the marks of his caresses and he realised he was actually not that exhausted.

Miranda threw a hand above her head and sighed. 'I really never knew that anything could be that marvelous, that I could feel... That was wonderful. You were just totally incredible, thank you.'

His eyes gleamed with warm amusement. 'You are very welcome and I can honestly say it was a great pleasure.'

'Are you annoyed?'

He turned his head to look at her.

'That I didn't mention...' She shrugged. 'You know...?'

Gianni lifted his reluctant gaze to her face—the shrug had made her breasts quiver and shift in a delicious way that fascinated him. She fascinated him; she really did have the most incredible body, so supple and smooth, she reminded him of a sleek little cat.

He couldn't look at her without wanting to touch her.

A faint flush had washed over her skin when she caught the direction of his gaze, but she had made no attempt to cover herself. The intense awareness of her body and the total lack of self-consciousness she felt with him ought to have clashed; instead, bizarrely and rather wonderfully, they complemented one another.

'That you were a virgin? It was a shock but, no, I'm not annoyed. Surprised...curious, yes, but not...annoyed. We might pretend otherwise, but it's pretty much every man's secret fantasy to be a woman's first lover...'

She rolled over, propped her chin on her hands and looked at him. 'Really?'

He gave a lazy smile and reached out to stroke a hand down the curve of her bottom. 'Really.'

She gave a wistful sigh. 'Well, when I find the man who fantasises about being my last lover I suppose I'll have struck gold.'

'So why was I your first lover, Miranda? Are you going to tell me?'

Miranda liked the way he had left it open, her choice. 'At school I was always serious, more interested in books than boys, a bit of a slow developer. Then when I did fall it was for someone who didn't know I was alive, not in that way at least. And while I was waiting for Oliver to notice me he fell for...someone else.'

The idiot's loss, Gianni thought grimly, was his gain. 'But you're still in love with him, this...Oliver?' She might be in love with another man, but she was in bed with him—the perfect scenario: sex without emotional entanglements. 'But not enough to fight for him?'

'You can't make somebody love you, especially when he's just married your—' Reluctant to reveal that the woman in question was her twin, Miranda left the statement unfinished and explained, 'He was my boss. I didn't want to see them...'

'Happy?'

Miranda shook her head and looked genuinely shocked by the suggestion. 'Oh, I'm glad Oliver is happy. He deserves it—he's a marvellous man. But I thought I'd sat around waiting for—well, I'd sat around long enough. It was time I did something—obviously this isn't quite what I had in mind, but I'm glad. Very glad.'

She smiled at him and Gianni felt a twinge in the region of his heart. Actually it was more like a hand reaching in and squeezing.

'To be honest I always thought that casual sex was, well…tacky, that it would feel wrong with someone you didn't care about…have feelings for. But I was wrong, it's not. It felt marvellous!' She pressed her head on his stomach with a sigh. 'It's perfect, really. We're both here and this is what you wanted, isn't it?'

She raised her head and looked at him. 'Isn't it?' she asked, something in his face making her suddenly uncertain of her reading of the situation. 'I'm not going to be clingy or fall in love with you, if that's what you're worried about. Most of the time I don't even like you.'

There was a pause before he replied. 'I did want this.'

'Past tense?'

'I do want this. Are you always this painfully frank?'

'No, that's just with you.' Which seemed odd, but now wasn't the moment to think about it because Gianni was kissing her.

* * *

The next morning when she opened her eyes the arms that had held her as she drifted off to sleep in the early hours were no longer wrapped around her. She turned her head and found the space beside her in the bed empty. He had left without waking her.

Startled and a little alarmed by how much she wanted him to be there, she reached out a hand. The cotton sheet was cool under her stroking fingers but the material bore the imprint of his body, and when she pressed her face into the pillow she could smell the male scent of his skin and the fragrance of the soap he used.

Her sensitive stomach flipped as she slipped from the bed, reaching for the robe that was looped over the back of a chair. Her expression was thoughtful as she belted it around her waist. So what next?

No matter what the answer was, Miranda found she did not regret the night before. How could she? It had been perfect.

Would it have been as perfect with Oliver?

Could he have replicated the wild and passionate lovemaking? It was a struggle to think of Oliver doing anything untamed or passionate, and Gianni hadn't just been passionate, he'd been at times during the night achingly tender and intuitively sensitive to her needs.

Feeling a stab of guilt to find herself comparing the two men, she released the trapped curls from the neck of her robe and let them fall down her back. You couldn't compare last night with what she had felt...did feel for Oliver. Last night had been sex—all right, great sex, but still just sex, not the deep and profound admiration and respect she felt for Oliver.

Yeah, Mirrie, but would respect feel as good as the sweet golden moment when you felt him move and...? She shook her head and closed down the line of thought. *Just sex, Mirrie. There's no point making it something it isn't. Just enjoy it— if there's more on offer.*

If not... She tried to shrug and simply couldn't even pretend she was fine about the idea of not spending at least one more night in bed with Gianni. The possibility that she would never have him take her to heaven again actually filled her with a sense of utter horror.

She showered and changed quickly before running down to the kitchen. The room was empty but there were signs of recent occupation in the dirty dishes on the table and the soaking pan sitting in the sink.

She walked over to the half-full coffee pot and, after feeling it was still hot poured herself a mug. She was taking her first sip and stretching to relieve the stiffness in muscles she had not used before when after a short tap the door swung inwards.

A hand holding a bunch of carrots complete with a ribbon tied around the leafy tops was thrust into the room before a hangdog-looking Joe stepped inside.

'A peace offering to apologise for being drunk and incapable last night. I was an idiot.'

Miranda took the carrots, but refused with a smile his invite to dinner.

'I blew it?'

'Not at all. I'm just pretty busy here and…' Her lashes swept downwards and she shrugged, smiling slightly as her eyes brushed the empty coffee cup on the table. 'It's not you, it's…' She stopped again and felt the flush rise up her neck.

Joe gave a philosophical shrug. 'It's fine, you don't have to explain. I knew the moment I saw you together there was something going on between you two.'

He smiled at Miranda's alarmed protest of, 'We'd only just met!' and excused himself.

Gianni, with a muddy-booted Liam and the boisterous pack of dogs in tow, appeared just as a subdued Miranda was putting the last mug in the dishwasher. She had spent the time since Joe had gone thinking seriously about his comments and had come to the conclusion that she needed to cool things down; she had discovered sex, not fallen in love.

She knew about love, and what she felt for Oliver bore no resemblance to the turbulent emotions that Gianni aroused in her. Forty per cent of the time she couldn't stand him! Having established that she loved Oliver and Gianni was just a wildly attractive man and a perfect lover, she felt her anxiety dissipate.

Then her heart almost stopped when she saw him. Dark hair mussed by the wind, he looked vibrant and so supremely masculine that Miranda didn't even attempt to play it cool. What would be the point? Just looking at him sent her hormones into overdrive. She had no idea what was happening to her, she just knew that she had no more control over it than she did the elements.

She pressed a hand to the wild pulse throbbing in her neck. 'You're back,' she said, sounding breathless because she was.

'Let her go, Liam,' Gianni said to Liam, who had attached himself like a limpet to Miranda's slim legs. He actually had some sympathy for the boy's instincts. The idea of getting up close and personal was pretty hard to resist.

'Can I play outside?'

'Yes, you can, but don't chase the hens,' Gianni yelled after his son. When he had passed through the door he turned back to Miranda.

His voice dropped to a low throaty purr as he stepped in closer. 'I didn't want to wake you. I thought you could do with the sleep.' He put a finger under her chin and tilted her head up; a slow grin tinged with a mixture of amusement and satisfaction spread across his lean face. 'You're blushing.'

Miranda snatched her chin away and fixed him with a reproachful glare. 'And you're surprised.' The things he could put in a smouldering glance could, she suspected, get them both arrested in some parts of the world. 'I've less experience at this stuff than you.'

'But you're having fun catching up, I hope?'

'Like you have any doubts.' She could still not believe the things she had said to him under cover of darkness, and even thinking the things he had said back sent her temperature up several degrees.

His rumble of amused laughter cut off suddenly.

'What,' he said, sounding grim and forbidding, 'is that?'

Following the direction of his dark and bewilderingly menacing stare, she saw the ribboned bunch of carrots. 'Oh, those. Joe dropped by and gave them to me... Sweet of him, wasn't it?'

'He has been here?'

She gave her Titian head a puzzled shake, confused by the overt hostility in his manner. 'Obviously.'

A muscle ticced in Gianni's lean cheek as a wave of possessive fury so unfamiliar that he struggled to name it washed over him. He inhaled and dug his hands deep in his pockets. A snarl of dissatisfaction rumbled in his throat before he clamped his white, even teeth together.

'Did you just growl? What on earth is wrong?'

Gianni's lip curled. It astonished him that she could ask the question. 'Has the man not heard of flowers?'

'Well, you can't eat flowers,' Miranda pointed out fairly. 'And it's the thought that counts.'

'I do not like carrots.' *Since when?* He mocked himself.

'Well, I'll eat them.'

'You accepted a gift from him after the way he treated you last night.'

'Gift!' Her brows lifted. 'A bunch of carrots, Gianni?' His belligerent attitude continued to confuse her. 'And he said sorry about that. What's your problem anyway? You're acting as though...' She stopped her eyes flying wide. 'You are—you're jealous of Joe.'

The muscles in his jaw quivered as Gianni lowered his lashes in an attempt to conceal the shock he knew he had not succeeded in totally controlling. Not that her accusation was true, though it was, he conceded, possible that he might have lost some perspective, but it was just so bloody frustrating that Miranda seemed blind to what he had seen within a second of laying eyes on the man. Under the affable nice-guy exterior this Joe was a wolf in sheep's clothing.

'I do not do jealousy.'

Then he laughed and Miranda immediately felt totally stupid for blurting out anything so ludicrous.

'You do know he's only interested in getting into your pants?'

She stiffened at the crudity. 'And that makes him different from you how?'

'You're comparing me with that sandal-wearing, beer-swilling creep!'

Miranda smiled and heard his teeth grate. 'That would be stupid—Joe is a great deal nicer.'

He snorted in response and scowled. 'Nice Oliver, nice Joe. Tell me, Mirrie, how come it's not so nice Gianni who got you into bed? Could it be you have a weakness for something that is not so nice?' He arched a sardonic brow. 'A bit of rough, perhaps?' His words were intended to cause offence and in this he succeeded!

Miranda paled in temper. Her lips quivered. She had been here before and experience had taught her that she was only moments away from tears and becoming totally incoherent.

'Go to hell, Gianni, you arrogant, smug sod!'

She almost ran from the room in her anxiety to

get away before she began to blub. Throwing one last look over her shoulder before she swept from the room, she saw him standing there with an expression stamped on his face that made it clear she wasn't the only one with a temper.

After a short, unrestrained bout of weeping she washed her face, went down to the kitchen and spent the rest of the afternoon making gallons of carrot and coriander soup and then a carrot cake. By the time she had finished decorating the cake with swirls of cream-cheese frosting she felt calmer.

Miserable, but calmer.

Gianni was avoiding her, and when their paths did cross—the house was not that big—he gave her the silent treatment, looking through her like glass. Miranda responded by leaving any room he entered, proving if nothing else that she could be just as childish as him.

It was Liam, clearly primed to act as a go-between, who opened the lines of communication.

'Daddy is taking me to have fish and chips for supper as a treat. He says do you want to come?'

'Tell Daddy…' She paused as a tall figure appeared in the doorway.

'There's an award-winning place about ten miles away. It's kind of a tradition when we come to stay here to go and have fish and chips.'

'Thank you,' she said, inclining her head with stiff formality. 'But I'm not that hungry.'

He shrugged. 'Rain check, then?'

She watched as he helped Liam on with his coat, knowing that by refusing the olive branch he had extended she had effectively surrendered the moral high ground.

When they had left Miranda ate carrot cake until she felt queasy and went to bed a little while later even though it was barely nine o'clock. She had not lain on the bed staring at the ceiling and thinking dark thoughts for more than a few minutes when there was a knock on the door.

Any thought that Gianni, driven crazy by lust, had been unable to keep away and had come to beg her forgiveness—the fantasy was still a bit rusty—vanished the moment he stepped inside.

His face was drawn and pale and his rigid posture was radiating anxiety.

'Before you tell me to go to hell, I'm not here for me. It's Liam.'

'What's wrong with Liam?'

'We didn't make it to the fish place. He got really hot and started crying... I think I should call an ambulance.'

Miranda was already on her feet. That Gianni was asking for help when it came to Liam was a measure of his concern.

'Have you taken his temperature?'

Gianni shook his head. 'God, that was so obvious. Why didn't I think of that?' he grated, dragging a hand through his dark hair.

Miranda extracted the thermometer from under Liam's arm and turned around with the news that the child's temperature was raised, but not actually that much. 'And now we've taken off his clothes.' The little boy, now stripped of the layers, lay in his pants and tee shirt on the bed, his cheeks still flushed, but he had stopped crying and he was dozing. 'I think he'll be a lot more comfortable now. Before you go to sleep, Liam,' she added, raising her voice, 'how about a drink of juice and a spoon of this medicine that Clare packed? That's it, good boy,' she said as the boy swallowed it, then took some thirsty sips from a tumbler.

She turned and found Gianni watching her.

'So you don't think it's serious?' He hated the feeling of not being in control.

'It's hard to tell with children, and I'm not an expert, but I think for the moment pushing fluids and keeping an eye on him would be more appropriate than an ambulance, but obviously that's your call.'

'I overreacted.'

She smiled. 'You were just being a dad.'

'Thanks, Miranda. I'm grateful. And about before…'

She shook her head unable to recall now what

the argument had even been about to begin with. 'We both said stuff.'

'So maybe we could…?'

Heart beating rapidly, she cut in quickly. 'I'd like that.'

He nodded, his dark eyes holding hers, an expression in the polished depths that made her insides melt as his gaze drifted to her mouth. 'But not tonight, I'm afraid,' he said, directing a rueful look towards his son, who was now sleeping deeply, before throwing a spare pillow on the sofa at the foot of the bed.

Miranda nodded. 'Of course. If you need anything…' She stopped blushing as she just stopped herself tacking on 'absolutely anything'.

The blush deepened as he purred, 'Oh, if I need anything you'll definitely be the first to know, *cara*.'

It was two-thirty when Miranda tiptoed back into the room carrying a cup of tea. In the bed Liam slept, his breathing soft and even. Gianni was on the sofa, his head on the pillow, his eyes closed, his face half in shadow, the strength of his stupendous bone structure emphasised by the light cast by the bedside light.

She stood there for a moment just staring, totally mesmerized, her heart beating hard in her chest. It hit her with the force of a tidal wave… She was in danger of falling for him. The realisation sent a rush of cold, clammy horror through her. She was falling for a man who had made it clear he didn't do love or permanent.

She sucked in a shaky breath… 'I won't. I can't.'

His eyes flickered open and Miranda jumped guiltily and almost dropped the cup.

'What did you say?'

Dear God, what is it with me? Can I only fall for men who are never going to be able to return my feelings?

'I wondered… I thought you might like a cup of tea.'

'No, thanks. Have you been asleep at all?'

'A bit,' she lied as she placed the cup on the top of a chest of drawers. 'He seems a lot better.'

Gianni nodded and held out a hand towards her. 'But I could do with company.'

After a fractional pause she took it and allowed him to draw her towards him, not resisting as he pulled her down beside him on the couch.

'Comfy?' his deep voice asked very close to her ear.

'Yes,' she whispered, feeling totally overwhelmed by the intimacy, the physical closeness. He felt warm and hard and so male, her mind closed down under the onslaught of sensory information. She shivered and closed her eyes as he drew her head down onto his shoulder.

'Relax, *cara*,' he said, stroking a hand over her

fiery curls. He kissed her closed eyelids and murmured, 'Go to sleep.'

'I can't.' Thirty seconds later she was flat out. Listening to her soft even breaths, Gianni lay there and realised that he had never shared a bed or the equivalent with a woman when sex was not on the agenda.

He shrugged off the stab of concern. One night holding a woman did not mean this had become more than simple sex. The lie did not come as easily as it normally did.

CHAPTER NINE

GIANNI caught sight of his reflection in the window.

It suddenly struck him, *Dio*, it was over a week since he had worn a tie! He could not recall the last time he had gone more than a day without donning his uniform of sharp suit and handmade shoes. Perhaps, he mused, he should instigate a casual day…?

A soft sound of amusement rumbled in his throat as he imagined the reaction if he sent a memo to this effect around the Fitzgerald offices. Or maybe not, he thought wryly. His management style had already caused a few ruffled feathers from the old guard, who had been highly suspicious of any change when he first took up the post.

When they had realised his slightly more informal style and the new initiatives he had instituted, not to mention the bestselling authors he had tempted to join them, did not equate with a lessening of efficiency or, more importantly, profit, he had been viewed with a lot less suspicion, but jeans in the office might, he conceded, be a step too far.

An office, he realised, there was no reason he could not be sitting in right now.

So why wasn't he?

Eyes filled with self-mockery, he shook his head and thought, *Like you don't know, Gianni.* He was almost running to get to the reason he hadn't packed his bag.

Real life meant he would not wake up with his arms full of warm, soft Miranda. The memory of their lovemaking that morning sent a flash of heat through his body.

She was the total essence of femininity.

He tightened his jaw and slowed his pace just to prove that he could, identifying the weakness that had made him linger here too long. Great sex or not, and that was all it was, the simple fact was there was no room in his real life for a woman like Miranda Easton.

Were there any women like Miranda Easton?

Pushing aside the intrusion of the whimsical voice in his head, Gianni reminded himself why this situation could only ever be short term—in a perfect world where he had not allowed his hormones to overrule his head it would not have happened to begin with—he had too many calls on him that took priority.

She took up too much space in his head. He needed a woman he could forget the moment she left the room and that was not Miranda.

Not only had she got under his skin in the short time he'd known her, she'd made him aware of an—for want of a better word—emptiness inside him that he had been blissfully ignorant of previously.

It was an insight he could have done without, but he felt confident that he could fill it with things that did not upset his careful life balance when he returned to reality.

The thing about Miranda was she didn't ask for anything, but he still knew that she needed more and, worse, she made him want to give more…. Gianni, always conscious that he was providing the love and cherishing of two parents, told himself he just didn't have it to spare.

It was tough enough giving Liam enough time and attention with the demands of being responsible for a publishing business at a time when the industry was changing. While he was not one of life's worriers, his father, who watched the progress of what had once been his baby like an eagle, was, and worry, as his mother frequently told him, could have fatal consequences. He was keeping enough balls in the air without adding another.

They were a total mismatch.

So why had he not walked away now that the

situation that had brought him here was resolved? Was part of the allure the fact she was something he could not allow himself?

He paused and allowed an image of her face to form in his head. Her delicate skin flushed with passion, her seductive emerald eyes dark and smoky, her full lips pouting. This was the way she had looked that morning as she lay beneath him, her slender arms and legs wrapped tight around him as she pressed her hot, sweet body against his and begged him to take her in a throaty whisper that had snapped clean through his control... Not that he had much control around her.

But he would, he promised himself. This had been a nice interlude but that was all it was. It was time he ended it... It was just a matter of choosing the right moment.

Miranda was in the kitchen where he had left her. Everything else had changed. He knew this even before she had turned around to face him.

He knew it without seeing what was written on the page of crinkled newspaper that had been ironed out smooth and spread out on the table beside the bunch of flowers it had been wrapped around when they had bought them earlier from the roadside stall with the honesty box.

He had teased her all the way back because she had put a five-pound note into the box rather than leave it a penny short of the one pound fifty request written on the board above the buckets of home-grown bouquets outside the farm gate.

She had given him a lecture on honesty that had made him feel uncomfortable that he had not yet admitted his financial situation was not quite what he had allowed her to believe. He was aware of the irony of the situation. Being rich and powerful had never previously been something he had felt he had to confess to a woman. A man most people would have considered experienced with the opposite sex, he frequently felt as if he were learning from scratch with Miranda.

He closed the door and she turned around slowly at the sound, one white-knuckled hand clutching the rim of the table, the other holding the printed page.

Gianni blew out a long sigh of resignation as she held out the carefully unfolded piece of paper to him in a hand that shook. The expression in her green eyes was a million times more condemning than the lurid headline on it.

He'd been waiting for the right moment—this moment had right and natural conclusion written all over it. He could leave now without any fear of her caring because she hated him.

He took the paper and, crumbling it in his hand, dropped it on the floor without glancing at it. He knew what was written there.

'I can explain.' He might be leaving, but he should explain.

Miranda's lips twisted into a bitter smile. 'Oh, that I never doubted for a moment,' she drawled contemptuously. 'You always have a good story, don't you? And me, well, I believe everything you say, don't I…?' The sheer level of her gullibility was staggering.

Gianni's grim expression grew concerned as he studied her face. 'You're as pale as a ghost. Sit down and let me—'

He sounded as if he cared… Everything about him was a lie and he was stupid if he imagined she believed all that guff about him kidnapping his son.

She wasn't angry because she knew he was rich and successful; she wasn't sick to her stomach because she believed the lies that they'd written in the tabloid scandal sheet. She was utterly furious because she knew that he'd kept his secrets to keep her at a distance.

What had he said the previous day when she'd caught him looking grim and asked him what he was thinking about…? *I want you in my bed, not my head,* cara…well, that just about said it all, and this revelation about his background and past was more evidence of his determination not to let her close. To some extent the growing physical intimacy between them had disguised the fact he kept her at an emotional arm's length.

She should run as far and as fast as she could. Why hadn't she before it was too late? Before she had fallen in love with him. The realisation that she was in too deep to turn back now drew a groan from her.

'I knew…I knew this was happening and I just let it.'

She clutched her head and groaned, hissing, 'You bastard, don't touch me!'

His face a livid white under his naturally vital skin tones, a blue vein throbbing in his temple, the muscles in his brown neck standing out in taut corded prominence, Gianni took a step back, his hand held up in front of him.

'Calm down.'

'I am calm. I'm totally calm!' she yelled back, levelling a shaking finger at the paper on the floor. 'And broke…' she choked. 'You let me carry on thinking you had no money when all along you're a F-Fitzgerald!' she bellowed.

'You're working for a Fitzgerald and I never made a secret of my name.'

'You never said you were one of those Fitzgeralds.' Half the books, no, more probably, on the bestseller displays had been published by the company he managed. Not only were they the most successful publishers on the planet, they were one of the longest established.

He'd even dressed, or rather undressed for the part; nothing could look less like her mental image of CEO than the man standing there in jeans, a shirt hanging casually open to reveal his gleaming, bronzed, tautly muscled torso.

The article had made clear that the man they were writing about had been born with, not just a spoon, but an entire place setting of solid silver cutlery in his mouth!

'Enough!'

Miranda didn't respond to the quiet voice of authority, but after a moment did succumb to the pressure of the hands on her shoulders. Breathing hard, her knees shaking, she sank down into the chair he had dragged out from the table.

Hand on the wooden back, he twisted the chair and her around to face him.

Standing feet braced, his hands brushing her shoulders as he retained his grip on the chair, his body curved around her. Miranda looked back at him, the rage and self-disgust churning in her stomach making her feel physically sick.

'You have had your say. Have the courtesy of allowing me my turn.' His clipped voice showed little emotion but the glow in his dark eyes revealed he was not nearly as calm as he was acting. 'It is true I am one of those Fitzgeralds, as you call us, which obviously makes me a monster.'

He had the cheek to sound angry... Miranda released an angry hiss of disbelief through her clenched teeth as she shook her hair back from her face and lifted her chin to fix him with a contemptuous stare.

'Go ahead,' she invited. 'I could do with a laugh,' she added with a bitter laugh.

Gianni tilted his head slightly in response to her comment.

'The story is dead. There never was a story,' he pronounced flatly. 'I have not kidnapped my son. I have legal custody of him and, yes, I know what it says there,' he drawled sounding weary.

'That load of rubbish?' She clicked her fingers.

'You don't believe it?' He looked bewildered.

'I don't believe everything I read.'

'Some of it is true.'

'Go on...'

Gianni nodded and settled back on his heels, balancing on the balls of his feet as he maintained the squatting posture that kept his face on a level with her own.

'I used to be the political editor of the *Herald*. You can check—it's a matter of record. It is also a matter of record,' he continued grimly, 'that during my tenure I broke a big story concerning a tabloid and some high-ranking civil servants...

Cut a long and grubby story short, some people went to jail as a result of that story, others, including the man who wrote that load of garbage, lost their jobs.'

His eyes darkened with contempt. He still thought that Rod James had got off easy but the man—a classic case of someone who refused to take responsibility for his own actions—had another view. He had been running a personal vendetta against Gianni, whom he held totally responsible for his fall from grace. On several occasions his desire to have revenge had led him perilously close to libel; this time he had stepped well over that line.

Miranda allowed her rigid back to relax fractionally. As she sat back in her seat she vaguely remembered the incident he spoke of. 'You were a newspaper editor?'

He nodded.

Her curiosity about him roused, she couldn't help herself. 'So you were a journalist?'

'I was a foreign correspondent for a news agency, first in Europe, then I was transferred to the Middle East. A big story broke just after I moved out there and Sam arrived. She was already pretty much a legend.'

'Sam Maguire is Liam's mother.'

An image of an attractive blonde floated into Miranda's head. Her blonde hair sometimes covered in a concealing headscarf, her full lips always outlined by a brilliant slash of scarlet lipstick, regardless of the circumstances managing to look effortlessly chic in her trademark fatigues and, when the situation required it, a bulletproof vest.

She was the sort of woman who defied stereotypes; the sort of woman who made normal females like Miranda feel hopelessly inadequate.

'Yes, the living legend herself. I was pretty starstruck when I met her in the flesh.'

Miranda watched his sensual lips curve into a reminiscent smile as he made the rueful confession and felt a stab of jealousy so vicious she had to disguise her audible gasp with a cough.

'We had an affair.' He knew now that Sam had been right: what they had shared had been fun but nothing serious or durable.

They might have drifted apart totally had there not been Liam to link them for ever. The romantic feelings had long gone, but not the hurt and the determination never to allow himself to feel that way again lingered. Because of Liam, Sam would always be part of his life. The infatuation had passed and also the anger that had followed it when she'd left him literally holding the baby.

Over the years he had grown to accept her decision without totally understanding it; he accepted he never would and no longer tried.

'Were you together long?' she asked, not be-

cause she wanted to know but for something to
fill the awkward silence.

'Hardly. A week later there was an armed up-
rising…a hostage situation, and Sam flew out. It
was a few months after that when I next saw her…
I was back home in London when she looked me
up.' He stopped, his eyes darkening as he relived
the memory; he had hardly recognised the woman
who had appeared at his door that day. 'I'd seen
Sam give an interview under fire—'

Which meant he'd been under fire too…in danger. The thought swirled in her brain like a silent
scream.

He stopped and shrugged, shaking his head as
he met Miranda's eyes and added simply, 'She
was magnificent, totally fearless until…the only
time I ever saw Sam scared was when she knew
she was pregnant.'

Hearing the depth of admiration in his voice,
she thought, *He still loves her.* The pain she had
felt when she'd witnessed Oliver and Tam fall in
love was absolutely nothing to what she experienced at that moment… It had been a strong
breeze; this was a hurricane. But then she hadn't
loved Oliver—that had been some safe little fantasy. It had taken falling in love for real to make
her realise this.

'When she calmed down we discussed it. There
was never any question—she was totally clear,'

he emphasised. 'She would have the baby but that was all. She didn't want to be a mother.'

Ironically his first published article as a journalist had been a scathing piece on fathers who would not take responsibility for the children they fathered. Society was a hell of a lot more tolerant of them than they were of a mother who acted in a similar way... When Sam had sat there and begged him to understand and not think badly of her, he had realised that so was he.

'I admit I really thought that after he was born she would change her mind, but she didn't.'

Miranda looked at him and shook her head. 'And...?'

It took Gianni a few moments to respond. The abrupt statement was more explanation than he was accustomed to supplying. 'And she...they do have a relationship. Sam is not a stranger to Liam. He knows she's his mother. Sam is involved...' As much as she wanted. He had left the offer but not pushing it; he had been elated when she had made the first contact. 'To a degree, but Sam finds older children...easier than babies...'

'And you don't have a problem with that?' Even if she had not been personally involved Miranda would have been curious about this unconventional arrangement.

Gianni gave a fluid shrug, his expression giving nothing away, but it was a subject where he had practice of hiding his feelings. 'Why would I?'

Let me see, Miranda thought. *She leaves you to do all the hard graft while she appears just when it suits her like a fairy godmother in fatigues?*

Glamorous fairy godmother.

'I'm the one who makes the day-to-day, practical decisions. We both agreed that it has to be that way. I'm the one there. Or at least the nanny is or my mother is.' His mobile lips twisted into a self-derisive smile. 'As you have pointed out, my parenting skills are not exactly brilliant. No, the problem is Sam has met someone she actually cares for, is considering marrying.' Considering as in she will; yes, he supposed, there was a time when the thought would have made him feel something. That time was so far distant now it was hard to imagine.

'She has?' Miranda's heart sank. Surely this would only be a problem if Gianni still had feelings for the mother of his child.

He nodded. 'To quote her he's…' his upper lip curled into a contemptuous sneer as he paused for dramatic effect before sketching sarcastic speech marks in the air and drawling '…the one.'

Miranda leaned forward in her seat and, chin cushioned on her hands, scanned his face, struggling to read his expression, wondering if it was jealousy that he was concealing behind his ironic grimace.

'But you don't think so?' She didn't need a crystal ball or X-ray vision to see that much.

'They've only known one another six weeks,' Gianni informed her with a disbelieving shake of his head. 'Six weeks!' People took longer to choose a new car. 'Do you think that you can fall in love and know you want to spend your life with someone in six weeks?'

Six days, Miranda thought as she managed a careless shrug and remembered that she had thought and said much the same thing to Tam when her twin had announced she was in love after her first date with Oliver.

Tam had laughed in response and admitted actually she had fallen in love with him the first time she'd seen him.

'You remember he was dropping you off when your car had broken down? He got out to open your door, so old-fashioned and sweet and...I thought that you and he were...well, you have no idea how glad I was when you said he was just your boss. Jealous of my own sister—can you imagine?'

Somehow Miranda had managed to join in with her laughter.

Gianni nodded, putting his own interpretation on her silence. 'Of course you don't, because you're a practical woman.'

Miranda was the practical one. Tam…Tam was artistic, much more of a free spirit—this was not the first time she had heard herself described this way. It had never hurt more.

'Sam was, but I suppose she is—'

'In love?' Miranda interrupted, unable to keep the edge from her voice as she thought of her mum's face when she had looked at her picture of the newborn twins and said with a soft sigh, 'It was love at first sight when I saw my girls.'

Poor Liam. He didn't have the protection of that special mother's love. It explained why Gianni was so protective. She slanted a look at his face, seeing not just the perfect bone structure but the strength of character.

She felt her throat tighten with emotion. Not only was he determined that his son would not feel deprived, but the boy was not going to hear bad things about his absent mother—not from Gianni anyway. She could not think of many men who would display this sort of restraint.

'She's talking marriage, so I suppose so.'

'I still don't understand about the article. How…?'

'The boyfriend.' Such a description did not seem appropriate in Gianni's mind for a man of sixty—a man as set in his ways as Sam was in hers. For Liam's sake he wanted things to work out. If Sam's life fell apart now God knew how far it would put back the tentative relationship she was developing with her son. 'He saw a photo of Liam and asked, so she told him that he was her son.'

And if he hadn't asked? Miranda wondered. How could any woman not be proud of any child, but a child like Liam who was so special? *If he was mine*, she thought, *I'd want everyone to know.*

'Isn't that good?'

Gianni flashed her a look. 'It might have been if he hadn't jumped to the rather unflattering conclusion that I had bullied her into giving me custody and deprived her of contact with her son.' Which to his mind begged the question of how well this man knew Sam, who was the last person he would have described as a victim.

Miranda nodded to herself. This was pretty much what the article had suggested with a few embellishments.

'But she…Liam's mum, she must have put him right,' she reasoned, still not seeing how this damaging and apparently inaccurate story had ever been allowed to see the light of day.

'Actually, no.'

'I don't see how—'

Gianni spelt it out. 'She didn't tell him. She was, she told me, waiting for the right moment.' Despite his amused manner, Gianni had not been exactly happy when Sam had rung to warn him of the offending article. He could look after himself, but the idea of the paparazzi camped on the doorstep of his home, Liam's playgroup, those lenses focused on his son, had made him sick to the stomach. And the possibility he might one day in the future see the article on some website made him want to ask Sam if she ever thought about anyone but herself.

He hadn't gone that far, but he had been furious and he'd let Sam know it.

'Just when is the right moment likely to be so that I know how long I'm likely to have rotten tomatoes thrown at me in the street?' he had asked at the end of his diatribe.

'God, you hate me and I don't blame you... You hate me. Alexander will hate me when he knows.'

She had started crying and Gianni had been horrified and willing to say anything to stop her. If there was one thing that he couldn't take it was female tears.

'Sam thought the boyfriend would be disgusted when she told him the truth, that he'd judge her.' He glanced at Miranda and gave a faint smile. 'People do. Unfortunately before she could work up the courage to come clean he confided the story to a friend and that friend turned out to be a drinking buddy of a journalist called Rod James, who has been looking for a way to screw me for years.'

'But you could have stopped the story or at least refuted it…?'

He shrugged. 'She asked me not to respond to the item.' Sam actually had a point. Responding to a lie would only give the story more credibility to those who would believe what was written anyway. 'She wanted me to give her the opportunity to tell Alex the truth and not have him read about it.'

Miranda felt her indignation rise. So it was all right for Gianni to read lies about himself. 'How long does it take to say I lied?'

He gave a fluid shrug. 'In her own time.'

Miranda stared, struggling to contain the sense of injustice she felt. He was so calm; he was acting as if that had been a reasonable request. Didn't the woman realise how totally unfair she was being?

'That's why I came here without telling anyone. The idea was to keep a low profile for a few days and give things a chance to quieten down. It seemed perfect. Lucy is the next best thing to a recluse these days.' He paused, tilted his head a little and looked at her sideways, his eyes moving over the soft contours of her face. 'And I woke up in bed with you. But you know about that.'

The colour bloomed in her cheeks. 'So you're not a kidnapper.' The article had not said so in as many words, but the implication had been strong, even suggesting that the police were trying to locate him.

He shook his head.

'Just a liar?'

Gianni winced and murmured, 'Harsh,' under his breath.

'Harsh!' she exclaimed. 'You let me think you were broke.' She groaned and covered her face with her hands when she thought of the advice she had given a man who ran a publishing company that had a dozen of the bestselling authors on the planet on its books.

'It seemed…convenient when you jumped to that conclusion,' he admitted.

Miranda stared at him in disbelief. 'I'm not even sure you know you've done anything wrong.'

A flash of impatience crossed his lean face. 'Is any of this relevant? I'm not a particularly nice man, but you didn't go to bed with me because you thought I was nice or worthy or that I'd lost all my money unless,' he suggested, arching a brow, 'it was pity sex?'

Caught on the defensive, unprepared and confused by him suddenly going on the attack, Miranda shook her head and was unable to meet his eyes. 'I've no idea why I went to bed with you,' she mumbled.

'Yes, you have, *cara*.'

Miranda swallowed and lifted her eyes. He captured them and he pinned her with a hot, burning look that made her feel utterly helpless.

'I just…you…?' She moistened her dry lips with her tongue and swallowed.

'You went to bed with me for the same reason I went to bed with you.'

Miranda despaired when the arrogant confidence that should have made her angry in fact sent a pulse of hot excitement fizzing along her nerve endings. His smile held a challenge she couldn't rise to because in it was a tension that made her heart beat slow, then as he allowed his dark, smouldering glance to drift slowly down her body she began to quiver as if he had stroked her skin with his fingers and not just his eyes.

By the time he angled his dark stare at her face, looking at her through the lush screen of his lashes, Miranda was so aroused that she could hardly breathe. 'Because we have a mutual…' he paused, his smoky voice deepening to a throaty purr as he put a finger under her chin '…hunger…'

Miranda swallowed. She was literally paralysed with lust… *Forget the love, just concentrate on what you can have, Mirrie,* she told herself. *Let it be enough.*

'You know, I think half the reason I didn't tell you I was not broke was it was actually rather nice to have someone want me for my body, not my chequebook, and to be honest I wasn't even sure that you'd ever find out.'

Miranda jerked her face from his grasp and shook her head to clear the sensual fog. 'Wow, that is honest!' she breathed with a whistle.

Gianni watched, the expression on his lean, sardonic face a mixture of wariness and frustration as she scrubbed her face with her hand like someone trying to wake themselves up.

'So have I got this right? In a nutshell you thought that if I ever did find out you'd be long gone so it was basically a win-win situation.'

He took her hands then in each of his and hauled her to her feet. 'It does sound bad when you put it like that.'

Miranda compressed her lips and refused to respond to the charm in his rueful smile. The man was totally shameless. 'It is bad,' she said, turning away from him.

Gianni stepped in closer. She felt the heat of his body before he put his hands on her shoulders. She turned her head, tilting her face to look at him, and Gianni could see the need, the apprehension and the excitement in her eyes. He wanted to be looking in those beautiful, astonishingly expressive eyes when he buried himself in her and felt her softness and heat close tight around him.

'So has she told him?'

It took a moment for Gianni to drag his mind from the hot, steamy place it had gone. 'Yes.'

'And does he hate her?'

Gianni pressed his lips to her ear lobe and felt her shudder and gasp as she turned her head to allow him access to her neck. 'Apparently not.'

Miranda closed her eyes, a violent tremor running through her slim body as his tongue trailed wetly over her skin. 'What about the tabloid story?' she asked thickly. 'Oh, God, don't!'

Gianni lifted his head. There were ribbons of colour along the crests of his high cheekbones as his glittering eyes captured hers. 'You want me to stop?'

'I want you not to stop,' she corrected, twisting around to face him.

His grin flashed white and fierce. 'Apology second column page three.'

Miranda, who had pressed her hands along the sides of his face, blinked, her lips an inch away from his. 'What?' She sank as she lowered herself off her tiptoes.

'The article,' he replied, bending his head down to her.

'Oh,' she said, taking his face between her hands again, but this time she made no attempt to kiss him, she just gazed appreciatively into his face, marvelling at the astonishing beauty. 'So you're not hiding any longer. You're free to leave whenever you want to?' The realisation sent a little chill through her warm body.

A furrow appeared between his brows as he slid his hands slowly down her sides, then, holding her by the hips, he dragged her physically into his body. She resisted for a split second before she melted into him, shivering against his hardness as he lifted her hair from her neck, his fingertips lightly grazing her ultra-sensitive skin.

'I suppose I am,' he admitted, wondering why freedom had never sounded less appealing. 'You are wrong about one thing.'

Miranda's eyes closed on a silent sigh as his breath brushed her neck, the words 'weak with lust' suddenly taking on an entirely more literal meaning—if Gianni hadn't been holding her she would have slithered to the floor.

'I'm not going to forget your name, Miranda.'

The way he curled his tongue over the syllables sent an illicit shiver down her spine and, *Damn it*, she thought, *he knows it*.

His tongue touched hers and Gianni thought, *Or your face, or your voice*. He deepened the kiss with a groan and thought, Dio, *or your taste!*

Instinctively Miranda fought against the current that pulled her to him. She broke the kiss even though she knew that she'd already fallen too deep to pull back in every way. She loved him and she always would and she'd take whatever she could.

Her eyes slid from the question she saw in his.

'I think you kissed better when you were not rich and powerful,' she lied. His kisses were beyond perfect.

Gianni lifted his head, resenting the stab of guilt he felt at her words. His resentment deepened, his anger aimed more at himself than her—didn't she realise that he had allowed her closer than he'd ever allowed any woman?

Even though he could feel the walls he had built up over the years crumbling around his ears, Gianni held on stubbornly to his last line of defence, telling himself that this was about emotions magnified by the isolation of the past week and nothing more profound.

'I don't know why you are taking this so personally…and it's not as if I share my life history with every woman I have—' He felt her stiffen and closed both his mouth and his eyes as she disentangled her slender fingers from his hair. He had known the moment he opened his damned mouth that he was about to say the wrong thing.

And yet you still said it, Gianni.

When he opened his eyes she stood there looking up at him with green eyes filmed with ice. She had put a few feet between them but an emotional mile.

She arched a delicate brow, her scornful smile hiding a simmering anger. 'Every woman you have casual sex with? My God, Gianni, you have a way of making a woman feel very special. I'm surprised you didn't give me a number to avoid confusion.'

His bark of laughter brought her angry eyes to his face.

'Have I said something funny?'

'Hilarious…you are nothing like the women I date or sleep with.'

'Is that good or bad?'

'Confusing,' hc admitted.

Taking some comfort, as much from his driven tone as his cryptic comment, Miranda studied his lean dark face, struggling to read his expression.

CHAPTER TEN

'MIRANDA, I'm going to go back to London in the morning.'

Miranda froze, her composure splintering into a million pieces.

They would never lay bare skin to bare skin again... Her sense of loss was profound; it had felt so right!

She retained enough functioning self-preservation instincts to bring her lashes down in a concealing curtain as she rocked back on her heels as though she had been caught by a sudden vicious gust of wind. She exhaled and lifted her gaze, a carefully and hopefully neutral expression pasted on her pale face.

Her body language probably wasn't saying casual interest, but if it wasn't screaming 'I've just received a body blow from which I may never recover', it was good, she told herself.

'You should try and leave early to miss the traffic. A light breakfast for Liam and, I think, take the ginger cookies. Ginger is excellent for nausea. The radio said there are still traffic works on the—'

Gianni, who had listened to the flow of information, suddenly cut across her. 'If you'd like I could come back for the odd night...?'

Miranda blinked at the abrupt offer and shook her head, her expression wary. 'What are you saying, Gianni, exactly?'

'I'm saying this doesn't have to end...'

Miranda pushed past the flare of relief and took a moment to respond calmly, reminding herself this was a reprieve, nothing more. This was still casual sex he was offering.

And she would take it because she couldn't not. Like an addict, she couldn't pass up any opportunity to be with him even though the constant battle to hide her own feelings was exhausting, especially when her hopelessly optimistic heart refused to accept that he wouldn't at some point see that.

'This? The fighting, you mean?' she suggested, adopting an expression of mock confusion.

'The sex,' he inserted, feeling and looking irritated that she had made him spell it out. 'It's good...' His lips curved upwards as he gave a small, hard laugh. 'No, it's incredible.' Why not let it run its course? Why deprive himself of the best sex he had ever known... The situation—

Gianni was reluctant to term it 'relationship' even in the privacy of his own thoughts—just needed… some fine tuning.

There was no question of him rewriting the rule book. On the important things he would not compromise; he would still be removing Miranda from Liam's life. The…situation needed some boundaries and he would put them in place.

Real life did not consist of lazy afternoon sessions in bed and late night strolls in a moonlit garden that was the stuff of holiday romance.

And holiday romance seemed an appropriate analogy for what he had been enjoying, Gianni realised.

It was self-evident to him, or it would have been had he ever thought about it, that the reason holiday romances didn't work when the holiday ended was that the couple involved were not prepared to adapt to the changed circumstances. They wanted it to carry on being sunshine and sex. His life was no holiday and sex had to fit in with his life; it had to be convenient.

Miranda took a deep breath and came to a decision—as if it had ever been in doubt—and lifted her chin. 'Yes, it is,' she agreed. Meeting his eyes, she wondered if the flare of emotion she glimpsed was pleasure, relief, a touch of indigestion, or none of the above.

God, if you want to know, Mirrie, ask the man.

Or are you just afraid of what the reply will be?
She didn't because deep down she knew that the
moment she revealed her feelings would be the
moment he walked out of her life for good.

'What did you have in mind?' Without waiting
to hear his reply she added quickly, 'I have a few
provisos.'

Gianni's eyes narrowed in shock—she had a
few provisos. This was not the way the scene had
played in his head. He regarded her with utter incredulity, the frustration burning in his belly the
only thing that made him swallow the scathing retort on the tip of his tongue. There was no harm
hearing her out.

'I can accept casual.' She cleared her throat.
'Casual sex, you know that, but I can't accept…'
She paused, embarrassed but not apologetic as she
completed in a rush, 'While it lasts I want this to
be exclusive.'

'You think I have enough spare time to fit in—'
He saw her expression and stopped. 'Exclusivity
no problem.'

'And no lies…' She was pleased she sounded
so calm and dispassionate about it all; her eyes
swept his face and she found it hard to gauge his
reaction. She cleared her throat and, adopting a
matter-of-fact attitude that she was proud of, explained, 'This may be meaningless sex, very good
meaningless sex,' she added, because this time he

had reacted, though the anger she had seen move across his hard-boned face remained inexplicable to her.

'But I need it to be honest,' she admitted, thinking of Tam and the on-off relationship with the slimy photographer that had ruled her twin's life for years. It was small wonder really that she had seen her salvation in Oliver, a man who was the complete opposite of her previous lover.

Admittedly they were not talking years here, more weeks, but the principle remained the same. 'I mean it, Gianni. As far as I'm concerned it's a deal breaker. You lie to me again, and I'm including lies of omission, and no more—'

'Sex...sorry, meaningless sex.' Again she saw the momentary flicker of annoyance. 'Is there more?'

Agreeing to something he had intended anyway required no compromises, so why not? he reasoned with himself.

Miranda shook her head. 'No, that's it.'

He nodded and she watched, not sure what was happening as he walked across to the fridge until he pulled out a chilled bottle of champagne.

Turning back with it in his hand, he tilted his head and said, 'Shall we toast our arrangement?'

'Lovely,' she murmured, looking at his mouth. 'But it would taste much better after you've taken me to bed.'

Gianni blinked.

It wasn't until she saw his expression that Miranda realised she had voiced her inner dialogue.

Gianni watched with a mixture of amusement and tenderness as the mortified colour flew to her cheeks and her eyes went as round as saucers.

'Sorry,' she groaned, covering her face with her fingers. 'I was just thinking out loud.'

He grinned and put down the bottle. 'Miranda Easton.'

She watched through her fingers, her heart leaping at the sight of the tall, dynamic figure striding across the room towards her.

Gianni unpeeled her fingers from her face, kissing the tip of each one before he pressed her palms together and sealed them between his large, capable hands.

The image seemed symbolic in Miranda's mind of his physical superiority and strength, a strength that she had never imagined could be so sexually arousing. The differences—soft, hard, fair, dark—between them were a constant source of fascination to her.

'I find myself liking the way your mind works very much. Think out loud as much as you like, *cara*.'

Miranda let out a shriek of laughing protest when without warning he swooped and lifted her up high into his arms. It was a token protest. She gave no resistance, just looped her arms around his neck and, heart pounding with anticipation, she allowed herself to be carried upstairs.

'What are you doing?'

Miranda slid her feet to the floor. 'I thought you were asleep.' She had moved his arm, heavy and warm, from across her stomach and he had continued to breathe deeply.

He didn't sound asleep now.

'It's eleven and I haven't bolted the back door and the dogs—'

'Why are you whispering?' he asked, sounding amused.

'I was being considerate—ouch!' Her hand shot out to steady the half-empty bottle of champagne on the bedside table, but not before some had slopped on the sheet.

'The dogs will bark the place down if anyone tries to get in, so come back to bed, *cara*.'

The sinfully seductive purr made it a hard invitation to resist; the hand that grasped her arm and pulled her back upgraded it to impossible to resist.

Miranda landed in a tangle of limbs on top of him.

'What are you doing?' she demanded, trying to sound cross as she slid her knees to either side of his iron-hard thighs and settled herself astride his

body like some ancient goddess, her hair streaming in flaming strands down her narrow back.

'I think I should be asking you that, Miss
Easton. You seem to be taking liberties,' he observed, staring up at the twin globes of her breasts
glowing pale in the darkness, the outline of her
nipples suggested by a faint dark blur. He felt the
inevitable lustful hardening of his body as he
looked at her. Where this redhead was concerned
he had never, on present evidence, had enough.

Gianni was contemplating sitting up and pulling
one highly sensitive puckered peak into his mouth
when she wriggled her hips and leaned forward
low enough for the rosy tips to brush his chest.

A deep shudder ran through his body as she
slid her hands, palms flat, down the damp skin
of his hair-roughened belly until she found what
she was looking for.

'And you seem to be enjoying it, Mr Fitzgerald,'
she returned, mimicking his formal tone.

Miranda smiled in the darkness and tightened
her fingers around the hard smooth column of his
arousal and heard Gianni gasp. Her throaty little
chuckle turned into a shriek when after a few moments of her ministrations he grabbed her by the
waist and smoothly reversed their positions.

'Not fair!' she protested breathlessly.

She saw him grin in the darkness and bend forward, then again he acted without warning, his speed taking her unawares.

She squirmed a little in token protest but in moments she was lying there with her wrists loosely held in one of his hands pinioned above her head. With his free hand he reached out to his right and pressed the button on a control that lay on the bedside table.

The curtains majestically parted, bathing the shadowed room with moonlight. 'Our Lucy, she does love her high-tech and gadgets, and, you know,' he drawled, 'for the first time I'm starting to think she maybe has a point.'

His heavy-lidded eyes moved in a caressing sweep over her body, her pale skin shining with an opalescent sheen in the silvered light.

Miranda, shivering, stared up at him. He made her think of some sort of Olympian bronzed statue come to life. He was so incredibly beautiful that looking at him made her dizzy.

Desire kicked low in her belly and she went bonelessly fluid as he fitted his mouth to her parted lips and kissed her slow and deep.

When he finally broke contact they were both breathing hard. 'You could have just turned on the light,' she whispered against his mouth.

He tugged at her full under-lip with his teeth, nuzzling the pink cushiony softness of her skin as his hands curved possessively over her breasts.

She shivered and gave a moan as his thumbs found the hardening centres.

'I'm a romantic.'

He was incredible. Through half-closed eyes she watched the teasing glow fade from his eyes, leaving a dark, feverish heat that made the muscles low in her belly quiver in an anticipatory response.

He speared his fingers into her glorious hair and sucked in a breath. '*Dio*, but you are beautiful,' he breathed, his expression almost reverent as he reached out to touch the side of her face, drawing a line over the soft down on her cheek.

Her breath by this point coming in a series of short, shallow bursts, Miranda turned her face into his hand, pressing an open-mouthed kiss into his palm. 'I don't know how you make me feel this way,' she whispered thickly.

'What way?' he asked.

'This way,' she said, guiding his hand down her body to the hot moist core of her femininity.

'*Dio!*' he groaned, parting her legs with his hand as he kissed her. 'But I love it that you are always ready for me.'

The feel of his hot body pressing down on her drew a mewling cry of pleasure from deep in her throat. 'I want you so much it's scary, Gianni.' Scarier still was the thought of how it would feel when he was gone, when the casual sex began to bore him.

Clenching her teeth, she struggled to push the thought from her head. Then he was sliding deep into her, filling her with his delicious hardness, and she didn't have to try. All she was conscious of was Gianni as they moved together in total synchronicity.

The next morning Miranda woke, her nostrils twitching to the unmistakable smell of coffee. Smiling, she gave a lazy yawn and turned her head. The bed was empty but there was a coffee cup on the table beside it.

Gianni made very fine coffee, but then Gianni did a lot of things very well, she thought, stretching like a cat and very nearly purring with smug contentment as the night came rushing back.

Great coffee or not, she would have preferred to see him lying in the bed beside her. She flipped over, punched a couple of pillows and sat upright. She took a swallow of coffee before pushing the wild tangle of hair from her face.

She had drained the cup when Gianni appeared. Unable to stop herself, she pulled the sheet up to cover her breasts. She bit her lip. The man could hardly know her body any better, so what was she doing? Perhaps it was because she had something to hide, something that she was desperately afraid he would discover.

She half expected him to comment on the ludicrousness of her action, but he barely seemed to notice. As he moved towards the bed she thought, *Something seems different...?* There was a lapse of a few seconds before she realised what form the difference in question had taken—he was dressed in a white shirt open at the neck and a pair of tailored dark trousers.

'You look…' She paused. Gorgeous, obviously, but she struggled for a moment to put a name to the expression on his face: not cold, not warm, but…distant. Unease fluttered in her stomach. 'Why didn't you wake me?'

'I needed an early start. There was no need for you to lose your sleep, too.'

'I'll make you some breakfast. Is Liam—?'

He put a hand on her shoulder. 'Liam is already in the car.'

Her eyes widened in shock, the shock quickly replaced by hurt he pretended not to see as he added, 'We've had breakfast.'

Miranda swallowed. 'You're leaving—now…?'

He nodded.

Forgetting about modesty, Miranda swung her legs over the side of the bed and released the sheet, which slithered down to her waist. 'I must come and say goodbye,' she said, looking around for her robe. 'Where have I put—?'

'No.' Gianni damped the beads of sweat along the rim of his upper lip with an impatient stroke of his hand. Seeing her sitting there, her lovely tight little breasts. *Dio*, a woman's body had never pleased him more, nor given him so much agony.

He had the control of an adolescent in the grip of a hormone rush around her, and why did she have to look at him with such trusting confusion? He was trying to make this easier.

Miranda looked up, her brow furrowed in consternation. 'I don't understand…'

'I think it's better you didn't say goodbye.'

'Not…? But…I…'

'You do understand that our arrangement does not include Liam, don't you, Miranda?'

The penny finally dropped. 'You don't want me to see Liam?'

He directed his gaze away from her swimming eyes only to find himself staring at her quivering lower lip. 'I think that is best,' he said bluntly, resenting like hell the fact he had to explain. She was an intelligent woman; she should understand. 'It wouldn't be fair to allow him to become fond of someone and then to have that person vanish… He needs continuity.'

All of which was true, so why did he feel such a bastard? He was looking after the interests of his son. *That's my job,* he told himself, and carried on feeling a bastard.

Miranda lowered her gaze and pulled her legs back into the bed. 'I understand,' she said quietly.

Her quiet dignity as she accepted his decision made him feel ten times worse, and ten times worse than bloody awful was bad.

'I hope you have a better journey.'

'I hope so, too.' Gianni hardened his heart and fought the quite crazy urge to retract his edict, if this was to work he had to keep the various sections of his life compartmentalised. 'I'm hoping to make it up on Friday night…?' A week without sex had never seemed longer. He had never missed the sound of a woman's voice and he was not about to start now.

Miranda looked at him as the realisation hit her that she was now a mistress. She lifted her chin. 'Perhaps you should ring first.'

He looked taken aback by the suggestion and by the queenlike dignity she had wrapped herself in. 'Why?'

'Well, I don't know when Lucy will be back. I might not be here and I wouldn't want you to have a wasted journey.' But he could spend the rest of his life kicking himself because he let the woman who loved him more than anyone else possibly could slip away… Yes, she would quite like that, she thought, pasting on a serene smile to cover her vicious thoughts.

Only it wouldn't happen. Natural justice was a cruel fiction, she thought dully. Instead he would forget her name.

'But surely Lucy won't be back yet!' Gianni protested, struggling to subdue a stab of something he refused to recognise as panic.

Miranda shrugged and fought her way clear of the fog of self-pity in her head. 'I don't know when she'll be back, Gianni. I've already told you that. So maybe Friday...?'

He nodded curtly and left without a word. She sat there listening to the sounds of him leaving: the footsteps on the stairs and the door slamming and the engine starting up, then silence.

Her serene smile vanished and she crumbled as sobs that sounded like an injured animal were dragged from deep inside her.

She wept for half an hour before she finally released her hold on the damp pillow and headed for the bathroom. She looked at her tear-stained refection in the mirror and winced.

God, but I look a wreck, she thought, switching on the cold tap full. After splashing her face with water, she straightened her shoulders.

'This is the deal, Mirrie,' she told her mirror image. 'So deal with it,' she added, pushing back the sections of damp copper hair from her eyes and pressing her forehead on the glass.

The option was... She closed her eyes and thought, no, she could not deal with the option yet. When it did end it would hurt, but she would cope.

Hearts didn't break and, anyway, those thoughts were for the future.

She straightened up and lifted a hand to clear the misted surface of the mirror before she picked up the watch she had left on the washstand. She wasn't here on holiday; she was here to do a job and there was always something to do…and doing was more productive than thinking.

CHAPTER ELEVEN

IT WAS amazing how much a person could get done when they wanted to fill every moment with activity. The place, already immaculate, shone. Every surface was polished, every weed removed from the flower beds, even the dogs' coats were scented and gleaming after she had spent hours grooming them.

She even managed to fit some leisure time into her work schedule. Though her first instinct had been to refuse Joe's invitation to join his team at a local pub quiz on Tuesday night, she had accepted. After all, there was no reason not to accept. It wasn't as if Gianni were sitting home nights pining after her.

She actually had a good time. Their team came last, but that did not dampen the light-hearted spirits of this non-competitive team who were keen to party on.

The effects of one glass too many of the local cider to celebrate the loss, Miranda had got up an hour later than normal the next morning and didn't even have time to work out how many hours it was before she was likely to see Gianni.

In the event it turned out that she saved herself a wasted effort of maths calculations, because just before dusk that evening as she was closing the stable door on Cecil, the aged pony, giving him his usual treat of one of the mints that he loved, a silver monster of a car roared into the yard, throwing up a shower of loose chippings as it came to a screeching halt a few feet away from where she was standing.

She slid home the latch just as the door of the car was flung open. Her heart leapt into her throat at the sight of the man who unfolded his long, lean frame from the driving seat. As he began to stride across the yard towards her, their recent parting still fresh in her mind, her initial thrill of excitement became interlaced with layers of uncertainty.

It was Gianni, but the man coming towards her was not the Gianni she knew. The car had changed and so had he and she wasn't sure what she felt about the changes. Not that there was anything to criticise—far from it!

Her heart raced as she watched him approach, struggling to see the jean-clad arrogant devil she had fallen for in this tall, dauntingly elegant and immaculately clad, expensive figure who oozed confidence, poise and, yes, she realised with a tiny thrill of unease, power. He wore it as naturally as the beautiful suit that was moulded to his equally beautiful body.

For a moment she struggled to see beyond the Italian tailoring of the dove-grey three-piece and pale silk shirt. Then he began to pull at the silk tie to loosen it and got close enough for her to see his eyes.

As she identified the gleam of raw need she saw shining in those velvet dark depths a wave of relief rushed through her. Unconscious of the soft cry of relief that left her parted lips, she began to move forward, slowing before she actually broke into a run in response to the voice in her head that cautioned… *Too eager, Mirrie.*

Good advice.

She halted a few feet away from where he now stood. She could play it cool; she just couldn't stop shaking. 'It's Wednesday,' she accused in a voice nerves had wiped clean of animation.

His dark brows lifted as he dug his hands in his pockets to stop himself grabbing her there and then. 'I was expecting a slightly more enthusiastic welcome.'

The sardonic comment made her feel even more awkward. 'It's nice to see you, obviously.'

It was not so obvious to Gianni.

'I just wasn't expecting you, that's all. You said Friday…?'

He gave a casual shrug. 'I had a meeting cancelled.'

Two, to be accurate, but as he had pointed out to
his PA when he had confronted her with his diary
he was not making effective use of his time. Why
have three meetings in three different locations
when the issues under discussion overlapped?
Surely it made more sense to combine them?

Not exactly rocket science and it irritated Gianni
that nobody but him had picked up on this.

In case his PA had not got the drift, he had run
a red pen through the two he felt could be dis-
pensed with that would effectively free up two
half days. When she had tentatively pointed out
that due to the late notice some of the people involved might have trouble adjusting their sched-
ules, he had retorted that if he could he didn't see
why they could not.

Feeling slightly guilty later that day, and un-
easily aware that he had been guilty of displaying some of the temperamental qualities that he
despised in those in positions of power, he had
made an effort to be less abrasive and had probably gone too far the other way, even admitting
that there were some problems at home.

He didn't normally take his domestic worries
into the office, but since they had returned to
London things had not been normal. To begin with
Liam talked continually about Mirrie and kept

asking when he was going to see her, unwittingly echoing the question that remained uppermost in Gianni's thoughts. Like his son, he couldn't get the woman out of his head.

Miranda, who received this information with mixed feelings—did him being here now mean he wouldn't be here at the weekend?—responded with an inane sounding, 'Oh…that's nice.'

He dragged a hand through his ebony hair and retorted grimly, 'Nothing about this week has been nice.'

The knot of emotions that had lain like a heavy weight in his chest since he had left at the beginning of the week had not, as he had anticipated, fallen away once he reached London.

That explained the tension she could feel coming off him in waves—a bad week at the office.

'Sorry,' she said lamely.

The awkward silence stretched and Miranda felt her resentment build. What was she meant to do? He knew about this sort of stuff but Gianni wasn't helping… He hadn't touched her yet, let alone kissed her.

Should she make the first move?

'I was just about to…' In the face of his fierce, soul-stripping stare, her voice faded. She stared at the nerve clenching in his lean cheek.

'What were you just about to?'

The sound of his voice made Miranda jump. Too

stressed to think of an interesting amusing alternative, she blurted the literal truth without thinking. 'I was going to have cocoa and go to bed.'

His dark features melted into a fierce grin. 'That works for me!' And he was beside her in one stride, breaking through the invisible barrier that had kept them apart. 'Minus the cocoa.'

Then she was in his arms and Gianni was kissing her with the driving hunger of a starving man.

A blissful couple of hours later Miranda laughed when Gianni walked back into the bedroom carrying a steaming mug.

He arched a brow. 'You said you wanted cocoa...' And he set it down on the beside cabinet.

'Aren't you having one?' she asked, picking up the mug and nursing it between her palms.

'No, I am not. It is a vile concoction and I do not have a sweet tooth.'

A tiny sigh of appreciation escaped her as she buried her nose in the mug and watched him over the rim as he unbuckled his belt and let the trousers he had pulled on before he left the room fall to the floor. She had never imagined that she would take so much carnal pleasure from looking at a naked man, but she had done quite a few things lately that had previously not featured in her imagination.

'It helps me sleep.'

'That,' Gianni admitted as he lifted the quilt and slid beneath, fitting his hard body up against her soft curves, 'is something I had not considered.' He took the mug from her hands and planted it out of reach.

'What are you doing?'

'I have no plans for you falling asleep on me just yet.'

Miranda snuggled in closer to him and lay her head on a chest that had the texture of satin and the consistency of granite. There was not an ounce of surplus flesh on his greyhound-lean toned body. She gave a voluptuous sigh of appreciation.

'Well, I hate to break it to you, but I can hardly keep my eyes open. If I'd known you were coming I wouldn't have stayed out so late last night, and the cider...' She shook her head. 'Next time I'll give that stuff a wide berth.'

'I am glad that you have not been bored in my absence.' Last night he had spent the evening working until the small hours so that he could be here this evening and now it seemed she had been out partying.

Miranda lifted her head to direct an enquiring look at his face. He did not sound at all glad. 'Is something wrong?'

He sketched a tight smile. 'Not with me. I'm not the one who's been drinking.'

'Hardly drinking,' Miranda protested, stifling a

yawn and missing the austerity in his deceptively soft voice. 'I had two small glasses all night. Joe had—'

Gianni swore, his accent thickening as, grabbing her shoulders, he pushed her away far enough to allow him to direct an outraged glare at her bemused face. 'Joe? You were with Joe last night?'

'Yes, I was. Well, not just Joe, the rest of…' She stopped and thought, *Why am I telling him this? Why am I acting as though I have anything to explain?*

Suddenly the utter inequality of this situation she had got herself into hit home with a vengeance. She had actually been on the point of apologising and for what?

She'd done nothing to be ashamed of except shelve all her principles. Because she had fallen so deeply in love she was prepared to do anything, sacrifice anything, be anything to be with Gianni. All the burning shame and frustration bubbled to the surface as she lifted her chin to a belligerent angle and pulled free of his arms, shuffling away on her bottom until her back was digging into the carved headboard.

Gathering her anger around her, as well as a handful of the sheet, she pulled her knees up to her chest and met his hostile stare head-on.

'I did spend the evening with Joe and I enjoyed it,' she announced, enjoying her residence in the moral high ground.

He sucked in a furious breath and loosed a short, angry-sounding Italian epithet.

'Is there anything wrong with that?' she asked him, ignoring the fact she knew it was dangerous to challenge him when he looked the way he did right now.

He vented a hard laugh. '*Dio*, if you have to ask me that…? Tell me,' he asked with the triumphal attitude of someone producing the winning argument, 'what if I had arrived last night and not tonight?'

'I suppose you would have let yourself in with the key.' It was still where it was the first time he had used it. 'You're good at turning up uninvited.'

His nostrils flared as he regarded her with a magnificent hauteur that his swashbuckling Italian ancestors would have applauded. 'You are suggesting I am not welcome?'

'I'm suggesting that you've got a damned cheek expecting me to sit here waiting for you,' she told him frankly. 'I went to a pub quiz with Joe. You're acting as if I've taken an active part in some sort of…of…orgy! And for the record if I wanted to it would be none of your damned business. We're not even in a damned relationship. This is just sex! Isn't it, Gianni?'

The silence that followed her outburst was electric.

On anyone else she would have called the dark bands of colour that outlined the crests of his slashing cheekbones a blush.

'You introduced the exclusivity clause,' he reminded her heavily. And he had not even demurred—what the hell was wrong with him? Why was he letting her call the tune?

'I don't expect you not to talk with women, only not have sex… You can't…just can't think I would sleep with Joe…? Hell, the idea of anyone but you touching me like that is…' She pressed a hand to her throat and gave an expressive little shudder before she could consider the wisdom of being this frank with Gianni—the last man in the world she would have imagined falling in love with and the only man now she could bear the thought of touching her.

Her guileless admission sent a stab of savage male satisfaction through Gianni. He gave a concessionary grunt and amazed himself by matching her frankness with some of his own.

'I do not like the idea of you being with another man,' he ground out between clenched teeth.

Miranda's jaw dropped in shock.

'Is that what you would call jealousy…?' he

asked her, the glimmer of self-mockery in his eyes mingled with genuine shock as he faced a fact he had been avoiding.

She tipped her head. 'I think most people would think so.'

'I think most people would also say we are wasting our limited time arguing.' He opened his arms. 'Come here.'

With a cry Miranda flung herself at him and felt his arms close like iron bands around her as he lay down, pulling her with him. 'You are so innocent,' he murmured, smoothing her hair with a tender hand. 'The next time a man tries to ply you with drinks, remember,' he warned darkly, 'you can't judge by appearances and many a wolf is disguised in sheep's clothing.'

She breathed in the delicious musky male smell of his skin, enjoying the moment, but still confused by the dizzying change of mood she frequently experienced around him. 'You're a font of wisdom,' she replied, her voice muffled by his chest.

'I'm so glad I amuse you.' He glanced down at her tawny head and murmured, 'Now go to sleep.'

'Actually I'm not feeling that tired any more.'

He placed a hand under her chin and turned her face up to him. 'Is that so?'

'I might not be able to sleep for hours and hours…'

'Insomnia is a terrible thing… You know earlier when you mentioned orgies? I had in mind a very private version, just you and me…?'

She looked at him through her lashes, smiling wickedly. 'I'm up for it if you are…' Her hand slid down his body and she pretended shock. 'Oh, gosh, you are!'

That first evening set a pattern that was repeated over the next three weeks, minus for the most part the major arguments. Gianni would turn up, generally without warning, two or even three times a week.

The time together was very intense. It frequently felt to Miranda as if they were trying to squeeze an entire week into a few hours. The Liam situation still remained a problem for Miranda. The first time she had mentioned the little boy's name Gianni had just spoken across her.

It had happened three times before the penny had dropped. She felt foolish that it hadn't earlier. She had foolishly assumed that he thought of her as more than a disposable lover, but she was wrong. He was still determined to protect Liam from her and she felt stupid for thinking otherwise.

The idea came to her when Gianni arrived while she was in the shower. It turned out to be a very long shower, but it made her think—was there any reason that she couldn't be the one doing the surprising?

She planned her surprise for the next Monday. She knew his London address from an envelope he had left behind and, while she knew she would not be welcomed there because of Liam, she didn't see how it would be a problem if she rang him from the hotel room she planned to book.

She caught the early train up, having taken up the offer made by a friendly neighbour to fill in for her at the cottage if she ever wanted a day off.

'The dogs can stay with me and it's no trouble for me to nip over the fence and feed the others.'

Miranda headed straight to the department store where she had booked herself in for the full works—hair, a facial and make-up. At the suggestion of the woman doing her make-up she took advantage of the services of the store's personal shopper. It seemed a good idea. She was wearing the only even vaguely dressy thing she had brought with her from home—the green skirt that Gianni loved—but he had seen her in it loads of times.

She wanted to show him that she wasn't all jeans and boots—she wanted to knock his socks off!

When she'd walked into the department store she'd had her doubts about fulfilling this ambition, but when she walked out of the changing room three hours later she hardly recognised the slim, elegant figure in four-inch heels and green silk shift dress with the Peter Pan collar—apparently the fifties look was very in. She'd never manage to duplicate the sleek chignon they'd tamed her hair into, though the bag filled with samples of make-up made her hope she might be able to manage something similar herself...though maybe not the red lipstick.

I'm hot, she decided modestly as she turned to get a look at her rear view in the full-length mirror, an opinion that seemed to be reinforced by the number of double takes and admiring looks she received during the short walk to her hotel.

When she walked into the hotel her confidence was on an all-time high that lasted right up to the moment she was inserting the swipe card into her room door, because at that exact moment Sam Maguire walked out of the door of the room opposite.

The woman was a hundred times more striking in the flesh than she looked on a TV screen. Not only slimmer, but taller and blessed with a figure that any catwalk model would have envied that didn't come across on the screen—nor did her height or her great skin. Dressed in a nude-coloured lace dress, high at the neckline, sleeveless and covered with intricate beading, she projected the sort of elegance that had not taken a team of professionals several hours to achieve. She projected happy, glowing confidence that couldn't be bought.

As she studied Liam's mother Miranda felt her confidence dissolve. Her outfit suddenly seemed contrived. She rubbed her hand across the red lipstick on her mouth. It was a look she couldn't carry off; it was a cheap rip-off—she felt like a cheap rip-off.

The other woman turned and, intercepting Miranda's stare, smiled faintly at her without, Miranda was sure, really seeing her, and glided down the corridor. She had seen her twin act the same way when on a visit to the States during the height of the popularity of the hit show Tam had starred in; she had seen her sister effectively filter out the stares of strangers that followed her.

Miranda, who had been mistaken for her famous sister during that trip and had hated the attention, had not been able to understand how her sister coped so casually with being the focus of attention.

When asked Tam had shrugged and said, 'You get used to it.' It had only been when the series had been cancelled and she had returned home that she had admitted it was the not being noticed that was difficult to adapt to.

Unable to resist the impulse that had her in its grip, Miranda pulled the card from the door and turned around to retrace her footsteps.

Is this how stalkers start? she wondered as she slid into the lift beside Sam Maguire, knowing what she was doing was not rational but doing it anyway.

The door opened on ground level and Miranda followed the other woman into the foyer.

She sat down on one of the sofas and watched the older woman, unaware as she did so of the admiring glances her own progress drew.

As she picked up a magazine to hide behind like some character in a spy movie the sheer lunacy of her actions struck Miranda. This wasn't curiosity, it was madness. She crossed a hand in front of her face as she experienced a wave of shamed embarrassment.

What had she expected—that the other woman would do something that would reveal what it was about her that made Gianni seem willing to forgive her anything? Was he still in love with her?

Shaking her head in disgust, she laid the magazine down and got to her feet. As she moved back towards the lifts she saw the other woman pause by the reception desk. She was speaking to a tall, dark-haired figure.

A stab of instant recognition froze Miranda to the spot. The man with his dark head bent to catch what the tall blonde was saying was Gianni.

Her first anguished thought was that he couldn't see her there!

Her second as she stared at the couple was, *They are way too close!*

The gut reaction was quickly followed by, *Don't be stupid, Mirrie.*

Considering their relationship, Gianni was bound to talk to her, and what she perceived as intimacy in their body language—the hand on his arm and the soft laughter—was just two people who knew one another well. While acknowledging this she couldn't help tensing as Gianni bent and kissed the woman's cheek.

Were they back together? Miranda shook her head and pushed away the thought, watching as they spoke for a moment longer before he headed towards the lifts, passing within a few feet of Miranda but remaining oblivious to her presence, while the other woman headed to the glass-fronted entrance, pausing before she walked through the door.

CHAPTER TWELVE

MIRANDA, who had held her breath for the duration of the entire scene, released it with a shuddering sigh of relief as the lift doors closed on Gianni. She was ashamed of her voyeuristic behaviour and cringed at the thought of what Gianni would have thought if he'd seen her.

Well, he hadn't, but he was here in the very hotel she had booked into; it seemed like a sign. Of all the hotels in London, he was here in hers.

She walked to the desk and adopted a flustered expression. 'I have a meeting with Mr Fitzgerald but I've lost the paper with... Could you tell me his room number?'

Her heart raced with anticipation as she knocked on the door of the suite she had been directed to.

When a few moments later he opened the door Gianni looked at her with an utter lack of recognition before his eyes widened in shock.

'Miranda?' A mist of moisture broke out over his body as Gianni struggled to contain the emotions he had up to this point kept in careful check; emotions that her unexpected appearance here in his world, his territory, had shaken free.

This was the tipping point, he thought, recognising that he would never again be able to pretend that all their relationship was based on sex… He had feelings for this woman. *Dio*, why had she done this? Why could she not leave well alone? Why had she pushed it?

'Hello, Gianni, I thought I'd surprise you.' Her smile wobbled as before her eyes his entire manner changed as though the light had been switched off as his expression froze over. She pressed a hand to her throat. 'Gianni…?'

'You should not be here, Miranda. This was not part of the arrangement.'

A cold fist of fear clutched low in her belly.

'But I wanted to surprise you.'

Inside Gianni's head a silent battle raged. Part of him wanted to kiss her, the other to push her away. If he gave into the former, he realised, their relationship and his life would change for ever. If he followed the latter it would be over.

So it was lose lose.

He allowed his anger towards her to build. This was the moment he had wanted to avoid. It was not meant to happen; she had crossed the line. He had worked really hard at keeping their worlds apart knowing that if he didn't he wouldn't be able to ignore his own feelings for her.

'Aren't you glad to see me?'

For a moment he didn't respond until he finally blurted in a raw driven tone, *'Madre di Dio!'* His voice cracked with emotion as he added thickly, 'You look—' He clenched his jaw and swallowed. 'This is not going to work, Miranda. You should not be here. I need my own space. I do not wish to be crowded.'

Feeling as if she were living a nightmare, she looked at him with hurt, bruised eyes. 'I'm not crowding you, I'm...' Her anger sparked into life. Why was he treating her like this? 'I even...where is it?' she gritted, rifling impatiently through the bags at her feet and grunting in grim triumph when she found the appropriate ribbon-tied container that was almost as pretty as the contents. 'I even bought this for the occasion, and booked a room,' she choked.

Tears of anger and self-disgust sparkled in her jewel-bright eyes as she held up a short slip nightdress, the silk so fine it was transparent, and waved it in front of him before dropping it on the floor.

Gianni watched, breathing hard as she ground the provocative garment into the floor with one spiky heel. Despite the situation his imagination produced an image of her wearing both heels and slip and nothing else. Gianni would have given a year of his life to see it for real. He clawed his way mentally out of the morass of lustful longing that submerged him.

'That was for me?' He swallowed hard. 'You got a room, you planned...?'

'Yes, I planned to seduce you...I spent half the day trying to look good for you...'

Helplessly aroused by the images her confession evoked, Gianni groaned before he shook his head. 'I have Liam to consider.'

She cut him dead with a look. 'Who are you trying to kid, Gianni? This isn't about Liam, it's about you and the fact that you're too scared to allow for the possibility it's not always possible to control everything. You won't let yourself feel anything...well, I think you do.'

Having vented her feelings, she stood there panting, her eyes unwilling to move on from the incredible brooding beauty of his perfectly sculpted face until, conscious of the familiar heavy fluttering low in her belly, she turned her head in self-disgust, leaving a bitter metallic taste in her mouth. *Get some self-respect, Mirrie,* she told herself.

'Miranda...'

She watched the nerve in his lean cheek clench and felt a rush of satisfaction to know she had succeeded in, if not shaming him, at least annoying him. Or was that pain glimmering in his eyes?

She didn't care, she told herself.

He dug a hand into his pocket and pulled out a handful of confetti that had spilt when the bag had burst. He had received a few dirty looks for throwing it over the happy couple outside the church; apparently he'd broken several by-laws by doing so.

Digging in his wallet and pulling out a wad of money to cover the clean-up bill was not going to be a solution in this situation.

'Why the hell didn't you tell me you were coming?' he muttered.

Dio, what a mess!

'I love you,' she heard herself blurt in a desperate driven voice. 'I know that wasn't part of our agreement either.'

He flinched. 'I'm sorry you had a wasted journey but this is not going to work.' He couldn't give her what she wanted, what she deserved from some other man but not from him.

He had to walk away.

Only he couldn't. His feet were nailed to the spot. He did the next best thing and closed the door.

Miranda stood there for a moment unable to believe that he had closed the door in her face, he had actually closed it in her face.

He had just looked at her and thought…what?

More trouble than she was worth and shut the damned door in her face. Anger got her as far as the lift, where she gave an ironic smile and sent a silent good luck to whoever came after her in Gianni's bed.

She'd need it, she thought, reaching for the hairpins that held the stupid new style in place. She looked ridiculous and she felt…

'I feel fine!' she announced loudly to the fortunately empty lift. As her hair tumbled down she brushed it back impatiently behind her ears, staring with a frown at her fingers as they came away wet.

It wasn't until she touched her face and felt the tears streaming down her cheeks that she realised she wasn't fine, and the way she felt right now she wouldn't do for a very long time.

It would have been an extraordinary gaffe if the Fitzgeralds had been allocated a table next to the bathroom or the kitchens, but the organisers were on the ball and they had been given a prime position, as befitted a group who between them were confidently expected to contribute a great deal tonight to swell the coffers of the worthy charity they were all here to support.

The Fitzgeralds were as well known in the charitable world for their generosity as their remarkable photogenic film-star good looks. Few people glanced towards the table without remarking on the latter tonight.

Natalia Fitzgerald, slim, poised, her dark hair shot with attractive strands of silver, rose graciously in response to the enthusiastic clapping.

'What did you buy?' her husband asked as she retook her seat.

She gave him a look of utter disdain.

'I dozed off,' he said defensively.

'Mum bought a fur coat for me.'

'Not you, you'd look terrible in it,' her younger sister said. 'It's for me.'

'Actually it's for Tia Sophia, girls. Don't worry, James, it wasn't real fur and it was a bargain.'

'I doubt that.'

Natalia Fitzgerald's dark eyes narrowed. Gifted perfect bone structure and flawless skin, she had not needed to resort to surgery to retain her youthful looks.

'You have a problem with giving to charity, *caro*?'

'Granted it is a good cause,' Gianni heard his grumpy father, oblivious to the warning signs, concede—some men never learnt. 'But could I not simply have written a cheque? Was it necessary for me to dress up like a dog's dinner and smile inanely at people I don't want to smile at?'

His wife bestowed a dazzling smile on a passing waiter. 'You think I look like a dog's dinner?' she asked through clenched teeth.

Belatedly seeing the trap he had walked into, the powerful millionaire began to back-pedal hastily. 'No, of course not, Natalia—'

'And smile!' she snorted. 'You have not smiled once, has he…?' She turned to her family for support. They, having been here before and learnt the hard way it was fatal to take sides in parental disputes, pretended not to hear.

Gianni, sitting between his sisters, smiled faintly as he allowed the familiar sound of mild domestic disharmony to pass over his head. Underneath the bickering he knew that his parents had a marriage that was rock solid, a marriage that had been strengthened and not weakened by tragedies that had touched it.

'No wonder there is a rumour you are dead or have become a bearded recluse.' She clicked her tongue with irritation and announced, 'You're just as bad, Gianni!'

Gianni's head came up at the accusation. 'Me?'

'Yes, you. You look like you're at a funeral.' Concern filtered into the maternal gaze fixed on the dark, handsome face of her eldest born, who seemed oblivious to the efforts of the titled beauty at the next table. 'What is wrong with you anyway?'

Gianni struggled not to snarl a reply. He had

come though he had better things to do—did he
have to smile as well? 'Nothing is wrong, Mother.'

The response was not sympathetic. 'In that case
could you pretend to be enjoying yourself?'

'He is enjoying himself, aren't you, Gianni?'

He exchanged glances with his father and responded to the appeal in James Fitzgerald's blue
eyes. 'A good evening,' he lied, thinking, *This is
three hours I will never have back.* But what did
that matter? What else that was more important
did he have to do with his time?

It had been two months since he had closed the
door on Miranda, and, while he recognised it was
a good thing, unfortunately appreciation did not
make it any less of a chore just to get out of bed
some days. His life had become a boring grind of
the dull and tedious.

'He's going to bid on the next item.'

The only thing he could recall expressing any
interest in had been a top-of-the-range motorbike.
'I am? I mean, I am most definitely,' he added in
response to his father's rolling-eyed glare.

'The next item?' his mother queried, consult-
ing the glossy catalogue in her lap. 'Are you sure
about that?'

Gianni gave a click of his tongue and nodded
irritably, attributing her question to her views on
the dangers of motorcycles. When he was a teenager she'd vetoed his request for the one he had

fancied himself riding around on during his 'rebel without a cause' period.

Dio, sometimes his mother treated him as if he were still seventeen.

'Have I mentioned that you look beautiful, Natalia?'

'No, you have not.'

'Well, you do you look—'

'Hush, it's the next item.'

In the periphery of his vision Gianni was aware of someone parade past them on the stage to the sound of loud music. Conscious of the paternal elbow in his ribs, he clapped along with everyone else, then sat back in his seat while some guy with a vaguely familiar face and oddly orange skin tones began to speak, pausing at intervals for the well-heeled—and for the most part drunk—audience to laugh at his jokes. Gianni's thoughts began to wander long before the speech ended.

What was Miranda doing?

'Gianni,' his sister snapped, kicking him under the table. 'If you don't bid you'll lose the item you wanted.' She elbowed her giggling younger sister and added innocently, 'Quick or you'll lose it.'

In response to the prompting, Gianni cleared his throat and said a figure. Having no clue what had gone before, and not wanting to add the accusation of miserliness to misery, he made it a fairly high number and hoped the bid had not already reached this figure.

The gasp that went around the room suggested it had not.

As the tide of enthusiastic clapping swelled then went on—would it never end?—Gianni glanced up without much interest. He actually was probably too old for the leather look.

The colour left his face as he surged to his feet. The violent burst of energy that had coursed through his veins like a blast of fire was snuffed out like a candle and he stayed where he was, swearing loudly enough for several people around to stop clapping.

He had taken a step towards the dais, his intention, though he hadn't consciously thought about it, to climb up there before he had realised that the woman standing there was not Miranda.

She had Miranda's face, she had Miranda's body, but it wasn't her.

Gianni had no idea how he knew this—he just did.

Gianni didn't give a damn that people were staring. He didn't care what a bunch of strangers thought about him, but there was his family…

'It was a joke, Gianni,' his sister Bella said when he returned to the table. 'How was I to know he'd bid enough to buy the building?' she asked, shooting a defensive look around her family.

'Don't worry, Bella,' her father said, patting her hand. 'It is for charity. A bit over the top, Gianni, lad,' he added, directing the comment to his son, who remained on his feet. 'Even if you did just buy a designer maternity wardrobe for the national gross profit of Britain on a good year...'

The words jerked Gianni from his trance. He met the query in his father's eyes with a stiff, pretty unconvincing smile and used the first excuse that came into his head.

'Cramp.'

The initial shock had worn off but he still had problem getting his brain into gear... The sister she had mentioned was a twin...an identical twin.

'Someone you know, Gianni?'

Gianni was able to meet his mother's openly speculative stare and say with total certainty, 'No.'

The woman who had Miranda's face was not Miranda. He had proof that was, to his way of thinking, more compelling than a DNA test—he could look at her and not immediately want to plunder those soft lips. Bizarrely there was zero chemistry.

'Pretty girl,' she continued, not looking convinced.

Gianni shook his head. 'No, not pretty, beautiful,' he corrected.

'Where are you going?'

'I made a massive mistake and I'm going to correct it.'

A sense of calm that had eluded him during the last tortured weeks settled over Gianni. It was as if seeing the woman with a face he had dreamt of had peeled away the last layers of self-deception.

Miranda, he realised, had been right. He was a coward, an idiot who had built the walls of his own prison brick by brick after he'd been hurt by Sam's rejection. He'd been so determined to avoid feeling that hurt again he'd cut himself off from the possibility of love, ironically in the process putting himself through weeks of pain and suffering far more intense than anything he had felt when Sam had rejected him and left him holding the baby.

Again Miranda had seen through his self-deception. He had been using Liam as an excuse for living in an emotional bubble.

'Wow, Gianni just admitted he made a mistake and there were witnesses!'

Not pausing to respond to his baby sister's sarcastic cry, Gianni strode away in the direction of the backstage area. Not many doors or curtains were closed to the Fitzgerald name, he mused cynically, not realising that it was the steely determination carved in the hard lines of his austere features and the aura of danger he exuded that made people hastily point him in the right direction.

He found her almost immediately. The person wearing the items he had apparently just purchased was sitting on a packing case having her feet rubbed by a tall skinny guy in spectacles who sat beside her.

He knew it wasn't her, but that didn't stop the resemblance hitting Gianni like a fist in the chest. *Not Miranda, it's not her,* he reminded himself. No, but the resemblance was spooky enough to hurt—a lot.

He made himself pause and consider the situation, the couple, because the body language between them made it obvious they did not notice him approach; they were too wrapped up in one another.

'I told you this would be too much for you, Tammy,' he heard the man say.

'I'm fine, don't fuss, Oliver.'

Gianni stiffened at the name. This was the man who Miranda claimed to love. He studied the unremarkable face and tried to see what she had seen in him and failed.

So much for sisterly solidarity. Gianni felt his hot protective anger surface as he stared at the sister's profile. He couldn't help the staring—they were the features he knew, the features that were burned into his consciousness, yet they weren't. The differences this close were subtle but, to him, obvious.

CHAPTER THIRTEEN

'CAN we help you?' Oliver asked when he had received no response to his questioning look from the tall, brooding, rather dangerous-looking guy.

With his air of restrained violence and the 'hard man' aura and the confrontational stare, he was the sort of person that peaceable Oliver would have normally avoided approaching. But he didn't like the way this character with the Adonis profile and the air of menace was looking at his wife.

'You're Oliver?' His hands balled into fists at his sides, Gianni felt a strong stab of antipathy as he couched the curt question. This man had captured Miranda's heart…what had she seen in him?

'I am,' Oliver confirmed, looking mildly bemused by the level of hostility in the dark stare fixed on his face. 'Do I know you…?'

'This is Miranda's love rat.'

It was Miranda's twin who spoke as she began to struggle to her feet; the man beside her hurried to help, providing a supportive hand in her back.

As she brushed down the creases from the Lycra-moulded fitted skirt Gianni registered for the first time her condition—she was pregnant.

Dio, no wonder Miranda had issues! He struggled to block the urges that made him want to yell at this pair. He needed information. They were, he told himself, irrelevant. The point was he would never allow anyone to hurt Miranda ever again.

'Where is she?' he said, scanning the duo with fierce eyes.

'Why? You want to break my sister's heart again, big boy?'

Oliver turned his horrified glance on his wife. 'Tamara!'

She tuned out her husband and lifted her chin. 'Well, it's not going to happen, mate. She's wise to you.'

'She is well?'

'No thanks to you, she's terrific. She's got on with her life. She doesn't need—'

'No, she's not fine,' came the quiet correction. 'Oliver!'

Her husband shrugged. 'Well, it's true, Tammy. She isn't happy. You can see it—she's bloody miserable.'

His wife sighed in agreement and turned her accusing gaze on Gianni, who was sifting the conversation for information he could use. 'And it's all his fault!' she quivered.

'Yes, you're a very caring sister. You married the man your sister loved.' Gianni waited for the shock to appear in her face; when it didn't his eyes narrowed. 'You knew?'

The guy with the spectacles shook his head. 'No, you have that wrong. I worked with Mirrie, we…she didn't—'

'Oh, Ollie…so sweet and innocent.' His wife kissed his cheek. 'Of course I knew. Mirrie is not exactly the world's best actress. I suppose that makes me a terrible person, but I'm not. And I'm not going to feel guilty for falling in love. Of course, I could have done the noble thing and walked away leaving the field clear for Mirrie. It's what she would have done had the situation been reversed, I suppose. But what would have been the point? That way we'd both have been unhappy.'

Head tilted a little to one side in an attitude that reminded Gianni painfully of Miranda, her plain-speaking twin continued to stare at him as though she was trying to make up her mind about something.

The silence stretched. 'Are you going to hurt my sister?'

'No, I'm not.'

'It's not me you have to convince, but for the record I believe you,' Tamara admitted. 'But then I have a very bad track record when it comes to lying bastards. I spent half my adult life giving my cheater slime-bag boyfriend a second chance and Mirrie was always there for me, waiting to pick up the pieces.'

Tamara glanced towards her husband, who nodded in response to the silent question in her eyes.

'Mirrie has another house sitting job.' She pulled an envelope from her bag and tore off a corner and began to scribble on it, lifting her gaze to the tall, gorgeous-looking man who was leaking impatience from every pore. 'This is the address. I forget the house name but it's next to the village shop. If someone doesn't rescue my sister soon I think she'll end her days in the wretched place. The entire village has taken her to their hearts. It's a total disaster.'

'And that would be bad?'

'Of course it would be bad—there isn't a single male under sixty who's straight in the entire place!' She poked Gianni in the chest and added darkly, 'If you make me regret this, so help me I'll hunt you down, and don't think I won't.'

Miranda narrowed her eyes and stood back, hammer in hand, to survey the effect. The house she was now house-sitting was in the centre of a village and her duties involved nothing more strenuous than feeding the three cats and a little light housework.

With time on her hands it had seemed natural

to become involved in the very active community, who had welcomed the stranger into their collective bosom.

'A little to the left, I think…' She adjusted the picture frame with her hand and let out a pleased grunt. 'Perfect!' she declared to the empty room.

Tomorrow it would be, fingers crossed. The village-hall-cum-tea-rooms would be bustling with life attracting, not just locals, but tourists passing through on their way to spend the bank holiday weekend by the sea. But right now it was a moment to savour and take pleasure from the results of the somewhat manic community efforts of the last few weeks.

The entire village had been involved, but when her expertise in the kitchen had been discovered Miranda had become the acknowledged 'expert'. It didn't matter how much she said she knew nothing about tea rooms, charity events and even less about health and safety regulations—who knew the hoops you had to jump through?—she was still considered some sort of expert.

So even though it had been a group effort she did feel a glow of pride looking at the once dusty floor now gleaming with a fresh layer of wax, and the windows framed by Roman blinds the women's group had run up using the bargain offcuts she had bought online. Everything on the freshly whitewashed walls was for sale—several local artists had been keen to take up Miranda's offer to display their works on the understanding that the church hall fund would get ten per cent of any profits.

Fingers crossed they would make a bucket of money for the church tower appeal, and it was an early start, she reminded herself as she pulled the keys she had been entrusted with from her pocket.

Lifting the skirt of her long dress off the floor— she was cutting it fine to be at the pre-fundraiser party, a 'posh frock' event being hosted by the owners of the local gastro pub—she headed for the door, poking her head in the kitchen, which was in the same ready-to-roll condition as the rest of the place, on the way.

Pausing at the door, she twitched a sweet pea in one of the fresh flower arrangements that adorned every table. It was amazing the talent that existed in a small community, and even more amazing what that community could achieve even in these cynical times when they pulled together, she mused as she opened the big door.

'Oh, my God, no…no…no…' She closed her eyes and opened them again. He was still there, not a hallucination—he was real. Gianni Fitzgerald, looking totally magnificent in full formal black-tie splendour, was standing in the doorway of a village hall.

Her mind went blank while her heart began to

hurl itself against her ribcage to escape the confines of her painfully tight chest.

She stepped backwards into the room and she carried on stepping until her back hit the wall. Spine pressed into it, she slid slowly down the uneven whitewashed surface. It was not an action of choice; her shaking knees simply would not hold her weight.

Having observed her slow-motion, graceful collapse without a word, Gianni reached out a hand, his dark eyes raking her face, feeling a mixture of lust—she was the most incredible thing he had ever seen—and alarm to see what differences two months had wrought.

What he saw increased his already painfully inflamed protective instincts. She was always fragile but that fragility was now extreme, marked in the jutting prominence of her collarbones and the hollows in her once plump cheeks. Her beautiful skin, white against the black strapless gown she was wearing, had an almost transparent look to it. He could not look at her delicious mouth without seeing too the fine lines of strain around it and feeling a pang of guilt.

When he recalled the shameful occasions over the last weeks when he had childishly wished that she was suffering, he felt resurgence of the self-loathing he had spent the last weeks beating himself over the head with.

Her weight loss was especially shocking, coming directly as he had from her glowing, rounded twin. He had walked straight out of the place and jumped in his car without even speaking to his own family.

He assumed the several calls on his mobile during his drive here had been from them, but he hadn't checked before he switched it off, his mind totally focused on finding Miranda, who, after her twin's comments, he had pictured living a mind-numbing existence in a rural backwater peopled by gay men and elderly spinsters.

The guy who had directed him here had been a thirty-year-old and not ugly.

'Cinderella, you will go to the ball.'

Miranda looked at the long brown fingers and swallowed, the convulsive action causing the fine muscles in her throat to visibly quiver. Sweat broke out along the curve of her full upper lip as she struggled to banish the image of those fingers sliding delicately over her skin.

'That would make you Prince Charming...' She shook her head. 'I don't think so.'

'So who's taking you to the ball, then?'

She ignored the question and angled a bewildered look up at the tall commanding figure looking totally incongruous among the chintz and china. 'How are you here, Gianni?'

He didn't respond to the question; he just tugged

viciously at the tie around his neck, wrenching it free so violently that several buttons fell on the floor, and carried on staring at her.

Miranda tried to focus her thoughts on the buttons scattered on the lovely, clean, freshly brushed floor, trying to decide if they constituted a danger from the health and safety standpoint.

As distraction tactics went it was a total failure!

She hadn't forgotten about the aura of raw maleness he projected, or the innate sexuality that oozed from every perfect golden pore. She recognised the sheer impossibility pretty quickly of forgetting anything about Gianni, but she had tried really hard not to think about it.

Now she had no choice. She could feel it—hell, she could almost taste it.

'I drove.'

By the time he delivered the delayed response Miranda had forgotten the question, but his voice drew her restless gaze to his face—oh, God, he was beautiful. The suggestion of levity in his response had not reached his eyes, they remained dark and intense, fixed unblinkingly on her face.

'Oh, yes…well… You know what I mean, Gianni.'

Her body language rigid with the pressure of the level of self-discipline required to stop herself flinging herself at him, she struggled to catch her breath as she drank in the details she craved before she managed to bring her lashes down in a protective sweep over her hungry stare, scared by the intensity of the hunger and raw craving that gripped her when she looked at him.

'Rarely, but I'm getting there, *cara mia*.'

The caressing warmth in his deep voice made the colour rush up under her skin. 'How did you know? I didn't give Lucy a forwarding address—'

'Oh, that was true, was it? I called her a liar.'

'You didn't!'

'She'll survive,' he said, dismissing his absent relative with a shrug of his magnificent shoulders. 'Your sister told me where you were.'

'Tam!' The ridiculous contention drew a snort from Miranda, who got shakily to her feet, still hugging the wall for support. Dragging her hair back from her face with one hand, she directed a scornful glare at his lean face, noting as she did the deep groove that appeared to have become permanently etched between his dark brows and the dark smudges beneath his eyes. She hated the fact she cared about these signs of exhaustion when he had probably had a great time earning them, she told herself, thinking of all-night sex sessions with his latest lover.

Even this masochistic assessment didn't stop her caring.

And nothing, she realised, would ever stop her loving him.

Her slender shoulders sagged. It was almost a

relief to stop pretending. What did they say—the first step was admitting you had a problem?

God, did she have a problem!

But at least she still had the support of her twin, who had wormed the story out of her, or at least the details she had felt able to share.

'She wouldn't do that,' Miranda said, moving her head in a firm negative motion. 'Tam wouldn't tell you…you don't even know her. You don't know we're—'

'Twins?' He had anticipated a little scepticism. Still holding her eyes, he dug in his pocket.

'What's that?' she asked, staring suspiciously at the scrap of paper he held out.

'Read it and see.'

Taking the paper by a corner, taking care not to allow her fingers to brush his, she took it, aware of Gianni's sardonic observance of the elaborate steps she took to avoid contact. She refused to look at him. Instead she glanced down at the paper unprepared to see her sister's distinctive scrawl. Her eyes flew wide in shock and hurt.

'Actually we had an interesting chat,' he said, watching the play of emotion across her face as she recognised the writing then read what was written.

Struggling to keep the doubt from her voice and a semblance of control, she levered herself off the wall and took a step towards him.

'I don't believe you,' she contended, stubbornly refusing to accept the evidence of her own eyes. 'You must have tricked her...I...Tam was—'

'Modelling some designer maternity wear at a charity auction—' He saw Miranda's eyes widen, her eyelashes fluttering against her pale skin, and added quietly, 'I was there, Miranda.'

'It was a favour. Tom, the designer, before he got his break he worked on her show...' She stopped and shook her head. 'You were really there?'

'I think that I might have bought some—actually, all—of the clothes collection.'

'You don't know?' He didn't seem to be joking.

'For about ten seconds I thought she was you.' The memory still had the power to send a rush of powerful emotion through him. 'Why didn't you tell me it was your sister who married the weird love-of-your-life guy you worked with, or that you even had a twin?'

Still turning the maternity clothes puzzle over in her head, Miranda missed the strained edge in his initial admission.

'Oliver is not weird,' she defended automatically, thinking, *And he's not the love of my life— you are!*

'If you say so.' Gianni shrugged his shoulders uninterestedly. In his view any man who preferred her twin to Miranda was a fool.

It had taken him no time to see that her twin

lacked all of the qualities that set Miranda apart from other women: the amazing empathy, the gentle caring qualities, the strength, bravery and sheer stubborn resilience and, of course, that amazing husky laugh.

'There was no reason to tell you I was a twin. What's wrong, Gianni?' she taunted. 'Do you have a thing about twins?' Her lips moved in a moue of distaste. 'You'd be amazed how many men share that particular fantasy.'

He met her eyes with a hard look. 'Actually I would not be at all surprised, *cara*, at the number of men who shared my fantasy.' It had been his living nightmare for the last two months that he had pushed her into one of those men's bed.

His dark eyes swept downwards to the smooth ivory slopes of her breasts where they pressed against the black satiny fabric of her low-cut gown. He swallowed. 'Has there been anyone?'

Part of him didn't want to know and part of him couldn't not ask. He didn't like the idea, but he could live with it; he had no choice. What he couldn't live without was Miranda.

'Been anyone…?' The penny dropped and she flushed. 'No, there hasn't been anyone. I suppose you've lost count by now?'

'There hasn't been anyone, Miranda.' There never would be anyone but Miranda for him.

'Oh!' The warmth in his eyes made her look

away quickly. Miranda couldn't allow herself to believe what that glow said. 'I still can't believe she told you.'

It was cruel! The recognition of Tam's betrayal was yet another layer of hurt on top of the hurts she was already carrying around with her. Some days while she laughed and kept busy, acted as if she were content, she felt as if the weight of the burden would crush her and she'd simply disintegrate.

'Or why she'd do it.'

His eyes scrolled over the soft contours of her face; he felt her pain like a knife in his chest. 'I would imagine that she wants you to be happy.'

'And seeing you would do that…?' She gave a bitter laugh and drawled, 'And on that humble note, what really happened?' Her eyes narrowed. 'How did you trick her?'

He recalled the expression on Miranda's more streetwise twin's face when she had issued her parting warning and shrugged. 'I'm guessing that would not be that easy.'

'Not like me, you mean. I was easy to fool.' *I started to think you really cared for me.*

He looked at the tears trembling on the lashes that surrounded her swimming eyes and released a hissing sound of frustration through his clenched teeth.

'You're fooling yourself,' he continued grimly,

'every time you get up and pretend that your life isn't empty without me in it. You're fooling yourself pretending that you don't need to hear my voice—you ache to hear it. Every time you pretend to take pleasure from anything you're fooling yourself.'

As he continued to outline with terrible accuracy and awful cruelty the way she felt, Miranda became paler and paler.

How could he know—unless...?

Her wide, clear eyes shone with tentative hope as they flew to his face. Silent now, he just stood there staring at her.

He smiled grimly at the question in her eyes and nodded.

'Yes, you little idiot, I know because that's the way I feel every day of my bloody life!' he snarled, reaching for her and covering her mouth with his lips in one fluid, seamless action.

Miranda's cry of joy was lost in his mouth as she melted into his hard, lean body.

The hard, hungry kiss went on and on. When Gianni dragged his mouth clear with a deep groan her head was swimming. Pressing his forehead against hers, he framed her face between his big hands and looked deep into her eyes.

'You have no idea how much I have missed you,' he said, kissing the corner of her mouth before trailing his tongue along the moist curve of her pouting upper lip and kissing the other corner. 'I was lost without you—totally and completely lost.'

Entranced to hear such words coming from this strong man who liked to give the impression of needing no one, she tugged gently at his lower lip before moving her lips along the stern, sexy curve of his mouth.

'Are you feeling found now, Gianni? I am.' What she felt, Miranda realised, was home, and all it took was his arms around her.

He speared his fingers into her lush curls. 'I'm feeling alive. *Dio*!' he groaned, inhaling. 'But I love the smell of your hair. I have dreamt of the smell of your hair.' He buried his face in her neck and turned his head to confess softly in her ear, 'You were right, *cara mia*, when you called me a coward. I was using Liam as an excuse not to become involved. I have been a fool. When I proposed in a fit of romantic idealism to Sam she quite rightly showed me the door or, actually, the tent flap.'

Miranda pulled back a little to look into his face. 'You proposed to Liam's mum when she was pregnant.'

'No, I proposed then as well, but the first time neither of us knew there was a Liam. I had a pretty high opinion of myself and I genuinely imagined that I was in love with her so the rejection…it hurt. So I just decided to cut down the odds of it happening again. I was so successful that I ended up living in an emotional vacuum. So successful I almost lost my chance at real love.' His blood ran cold when he thought how close he had come to blowing it all. 'You are my soul mate, Miranda. I truly believe that.'

Moved to tears by his husky sincerity, Miranda took his hand and pressed it to her lips, a furrow appearing on her brow as she noticed the marks on his knuckles. 'What did you do there? Have you been fighting?' she asked, her protective hackles rising as she imagined him fending off armed assailants and fighting for his life.

'Only with myself,' he admitted, glancing down at his hand before smoothing her hair from her face.

'How do you mean?'

'After I closed the door on you I…' He gave an embarrassed grimace. 'I punched the wall… Look, I know, not a clever thing to do, and don't worry I paid for the damage, but the cuts—I should have had them cleaned. They got infected…'

'You punched the wall?' she echoed in total amazement.

'All right, I'm not proud of it—actually I'm not proud of anything I did that day. You were right—every word you said was true and deep down I knew it. I think I've loved you almost from day one but I was still in denial.'

Gianni lifted the mass of fiery curls, exposing the nape of her neck. She shivered, a rash of goose bumps erupting over her entire body as his fingertips glided in a series of arabesques over her skin.

'Do you still have feelings for Sam? I know she's part of your life because of Liam but—'

'Yes, she is part of my life, but if Liam hadn't happened I wouldn't even be able to recall the colour of her eyes or the sound of her voice today. I'll never forget your eyes or your voice, Miranda.

'And it's just as well I don't carry a torch for Sam because that day at the hotel she'd just been married.'

'She married Alexander...you met him?'

'I wasn't going to allow Liam to spend time with someone I hadn't met, regardless of whether the vetting process didn't reveal any dark secrets.' He slid his hands into her hair and tugged, sliding his fingers around the lovely curve of her jaw to angle her face up to his.

'You had him vetted?'

'I have everyone who comes into contact with Liam vetted.'

'Me?'

He shook his head and looked at her with such tenderness that Miranda filled up again. 'I always make exceptions for women I find in my bed, *cara*.'

The dimple in her cheek deepened. 'My bed.'

He tipped his dark head meekly. 'I could argue and say it was actually Lucy's bed...'

'But that,' she inserted, widening her eyes innocently, 'would be so unlike you.'

He grinned, the laughter dying from his eyes as he declared fiercely, 'You were perfect.'

'That's not what you said.'

'What can I say? Falling in love with a beautiful red-headed witch was not in my five-year plan... I was an idiot. I was trying to fight fate when I should have been enjoying what it had given me.'

She touched his face, getting a little thrill from just knowing she could. 'I thought you were a dream when I first saw you... You were just too perfect to be true,' she mused, dragging her fingertips down the rough stubble on his jaw and feeling the gentle kick of lust low in her belly.

'So did this Alex pass the Gianni test?'

'He's all right, and they seem good together, which is just as well given they got married.'

She stepped into him, tilting her face up to his as she began to run her hands up and down his arms in a slow, caressing sweep, loving the feel of the coiled, hard strength.

He tilted his head to brush the hand that briefly lay on his shoulder with his cheek. 'If you'd got there five minutes earlier you'd have seen Liam in his pageboy outfit. One thing, Miranda—as much as I love you, if you want him to wear one of those things for our wedding you can get him into it because I'm not going there again!' he declared with feeling. 'No way!'

Her roaming hands stilled, tightening over the bulging muscles of his upper arms hard enough to draw a questioning glance from Gianni.

'Are you all right…?' he asked, anxiety sharpening his voice. 'You look…?'

'Our wedding?'

He relaxed fractionally, but remained confused by her astonished expression.

'Well, what else did you think this was all about?'

He sounded astounded, which was so, she thought ruefully, like Gianni. 'You want to marry me?'

'Of course. Don't you want to marry me?'

She arched a brow. 'And if I said no…?'

He tilted his head and adopted an attitude of mock offence. 'I'd respect your wishes.'

She let out a hoot of laughter. 'You liar!'

His white wolfish grin flashed. 'Well, I'd continue to ask until you said yes, but very respectfully.' He gave a careless shrug. 'Which amounts to the same thing.'

'You're impossible.' Miranda laughed. 'But I love you.'

'And I love you!' he declared, fitting his mouth to hers, kissing her with a desperation that awoke a similar need in Miranda. Several steamy minutes later they came up for air.

He smiled down into her passion-flushed face. 'So is that a yes?'

'You haven't asked me yet,' she teasingly reminded.

'You want a proposal…right…I can do that…'

'No, it's fine,' she said, laughing as he gathered her hands in his and pressed them against his chest over his heart.

'Hush, I want to do this,' he chided, silencing her with a gentle brush of his lips. 'You once said to me, Miranda, that you were holding out for a man whose fantasy was to be your last lover and not your first.' Holding her eyes, he lifted her hands to his lips. 'Well, I was your first lover and it would be my honour and, yes, quite definitely my fantasy, to be your last lover. Will you marry me, Miranda Easton? Are those happy tears…? I hope?' he added, touching a teardrop running down her smooth cheek.

She nodded and looked up at him with love shining in her eyes like stars. 'Yes, Gianni,' she promised in a voice thick with emotional tears. 'Very happy and, yes, I would love to be your wife.'

'And you don't mind that we come as a package deal, Liam and I?'

Miranda laughed at the question and blotted the

moisture on her cheeks with the back of her hand. 'That's not a serious question, is it?' She sniffed. 'I love Liam.'

'And he loves you—the little monster never stops talking about you...' Taking her hand, he directed a critical look around the room as though seeing his surroundings for the first time. 'What is this place?'

'It's the—oh, God!' she gasped. 'I should have been at the party ages ago...'

Gianni's hands fell heavily on her shoulders. He shook his head. 'No!'

'No?'

'The only party we are having is one for two people,' he said, pointing from her chest to his. 'Us.' The passionate intensity in his unambiguously carnal stare made the muscles low in her pelvis quiver violently in response. The bodice of her dress chafed against her peaking nipples. 'In order to preserve what little sanity I have left I need to spend the next day making love to you.'

Miranda ran her tongue across her dry lips. 'I suppose nobody will notice I'm not there... I'm staying in...'

'No!'

She blinked. 'You're being very masterful!'

'I hope that was not a criticism, although you have to agree, I think, *cara*, that I have no problem with role reversal if the occasion requires it,' he teased with a slow sardonic smile. '*Dio*, but I love it when you blush!' he breathed. 'I am tired of spending our nights in someone else's bed. Tonight we will go back to London. Liam is staying with his grandmother for the weekend. We will have the place to ourselves. Then tomorrow...' his smoky stare slid to her lips '...or maybe the next day we will go looking for a house in which we can put our bed.'

Miranda was fascinated by the plan. 'Just like that.'

'Certainly just like that. Your problem, Miranda, is you make problems where there are none.'

'But I'm house sitting. I'm meant to be here tomorrow. People expect—'

'Details. I will sort everything out—leave it to me. You don't think I am able?' he challenged.

'I know you're able,' she admitted, discovering she was extremely tempted by the idea of offloading her responsibilities on to his shoulders—they were very broad shoulders.

He lifted a sardonic brow. 'And I have a very nice bed...most capacious...'

With a smile Miranda took a step towards the door before she looked back over her shoulder. 'What are you waiting for?'

He was at her side in an instant. She took him by the lapels and stretched up to press a long, lingering kiss on his lips. 'Gianni, I don't care if I spend the night on bare boards so long as I spend it with you! I can't wait to start living the rest of my life with you.'

His eyes glowed with fierce love and possessive pride as he looked down into the beautiful face of the woman he was going to spend his life waking up next to. 'As my wife.'

'As your wife.'

'How does next week sound?'

CHAPTER FOURTEEN

MIRANDA had assumed Gianni was joking, but he hadn't been. They had reached a compromise. It was four weeks later that they stood in the small village church where her parents had been married and exchanged their vows.

Miranda had walked the short distance to the church with her father. She made the return journey beside Gianni in the classic convertible he had arrived in with his best man, who ran behind them all the way back with Liam dressed in a pirate costume—his choice—on his shoulders.

They did not need the roof. The late September sun had shone benignly down on them. In fact the day had been perfect in every detail, the relaxed country wedding that Miranda had secretly always dreamed of having.

From the flower-filled courtyard by the stables, dressed for the occasion with zinc tubs crammed with sweet-smelling late summer roses, where their guests had drunk champagne, they had all moved to the marquee that had been erected in the orchard, led by sword-waving Liam in his pirate costume throwing handfuls of rose petals at the feet of his dad and new mum.

Miranda's mother had taken personal charge of the décor, keeping everything simple and rustic, laying the long tables with white cloths embellished with arrangements of flowers from her garden and long strands of ivy.

The day had passed in a happy blur for Miranda, who wore a vintage dress that had belonged to her great-grandmother and a veil that Gianni's mother had been married in. Her sister, glowing in a blue silk dress she said made her look like a barrage balloon, had stood as her maid of honour and spent the entire day smiling except for the one moment, rather to Miranda's mystification, when she had turned to Gianni and wagged her finger, saying sternly, 'I meant it, big boy!'

'What did she mean?' Miranda had asked.

Gianni had promised to tell her later but he hadn't. There had been too many people who wanted to speak to them both, too many people who wanted to wish them well. Lucy, who had arrived looking incredibly beautiful and happy—the tall, handsome Spaniard she had in tow might, Miranda suspected, have something to do with that—had given her an especially warm hug.

As the day lengthened and the sun vanished

the scene took on a fairy-tale atmosphere illuminated by strings of white light and lanterns hung from the trees. The braziers had been lit and the guests danced long into the night, long after the bride and groom had vanished.

They spent the first two weeks of their honeymoon alone in a gorgeous sugar-pink villa with breathtaking views on the Amalfi coast, before Liam arrived with both Gianni's and Miranda's parents and they all spent the following two weeks there.

'So back to the real world,' Gianni observed, sending a sideways glance towards his wife as they drove from the airport. 'A grindstone with my name on it awaits.'

Miranda nodded. In her view any world with her gorgeous husband in it was pretty special.

'We're going the wrong way,' she realised, catching sight of a sign on the small road they had turned onto.

'I wondered when you'd realise. That house we never got to find—I thought we should start looking again.'

'Now?' said Miranda, glancing at Liam dozing in the back seat. They had taken every precaution possible to prevent his travel sickness, but a car journey straight on top of the flight seemed to be pushing their luck to her.

Clearly Gianni thought differently.

'Seemed as good a time as any, but don't worry, we're here,' he announced, turning into a gated driveway.

'I hate to break it to you, Gianni, but this is the one we saw that first day—the one that was too big and falling down.' A total wreck, had been his verdict.

'You sure?'

'Positive. They've done some work on the entrance and the drive, but it's definitely the same place.'

'Would that be the one that had ten bedrooms? Half a roof and a meadow where the lawn once was? The place with all the original features you were so enthused about and the grave dedicated to a long-dead family pet under a fig tree in the walled garden, which for some inexplicable reason made you weep.'

'There's no need to be nasty just because you made a mistake...and there was not half a roof. There were a few holes, admittedly, but—oh, my giddy aunt.' She gasped as they rounded the bend in the drive and the house came into view.

'Welcome to your new home, Mrs Fitzgerald,' he said, bringing the car to a halt on the gravelled forecourt that had not previously been there.

She looked at him with big eyes, then back at

the pristine and perfect façade, not a broken pane or patch of peeling paint in sight. 'Seriously?'

'Seriously,' he said, watching her face with a smile.

'But how—how on earth did you do all this? It was…' She shook her head, lost for adequate words to describe the transformation.

'I put in an offer the day we saw it,' he revealed, enjoying the look of astonishment on her face. 'Actually the basic structure was sound and you can achieve a lot in eight weeks.' Especially when you had teams working round the clock.

'It's a miracle!' she cried, throwing herself at him.

'You're the miracle, Miranda,' Gianni said, returning her kiss with equal enthusiasm.

'I would live in a tent with you, Gianni,' she told him fiercely.

'Not practical, but I'm touched.'

'It's such a big house, Gianni, though…' She sucked in a happy little breath and shot him an almost shy look through her lashes. 'Maybe a tent wouldn't be practical. I was planning on telling you tonight, but, well…we might need another of those rooms.'

He realised what she was saying right away; his face lit up with delight. His eyes went to her stomach.

'A spring baby,' she said in answer to his silent question. 'March, if my dates are right.'

'I want a brother.'

They both turned, laughing, in the direction of the voice that came from the back seat.

'Well, champ, you have to pretty much take what you're given, but my motto is if at first you don't succeed, try try again... Does that work for you, *cara mia*?'

'Oh, Gianni,' she said mistily. 'I love you so much I can't believe I can be this happy.'

'I want to call him Spot!'

They exchanged glances. 'Interesting choice, Liam,' his father said, murmuring under his breath to Miranda, 'You going to break it to him or shall I?'

'Hush,' she hissed back as she opened the car door. 'He'll change his mind. Come on, Liam, let's go pick out your new room.'

'Can I pick out Spot's room too?'

'Yes, you can pick out Spot's room, darling,' Miranda promised as the little boy skipped up to his new home between his parents. At the door he turned around.

'Will you two stop kissing?'

'No,' said his father, not prepared to humour his son on this point. 'Not in this lifetime anyway,' he added, scooping his wife up into his arms. 'It is tradition.'

She gave a contented sigh and whispered in his ear, 'Not in any lifetime, my love.'

Miranda had found her soul mate and she was not letting go—ever!

* * * * *